BEST FRIEND'S BIG BROTHER

Older Man Younger Woman Romance

J. P. COMEAU

I

Margo

The Miami Beach sunrise was bright enough to awaken me long before my alarm clock went off. My fresh, crisp sheets were pulled up to my neck as I glanced out the window. Living close to the beach blessed me with breathtaking views directly from my bed, which was why I had positioned it so close to the window. I wanted to both see and hear the waves crashing against the shore first thing in the morning.

The view was the only thing keeping me from having a mental breakdown that morning too.

My feet hit the rug as I made my way into the bathroom to get ready for work, stopping along the way to chuck one of Nick's T-shirts into the kitchen garbage. What a waste of time that relationship had been. He finally had the balls to end it after three months of stringing me along, but the jerk dared to do so right before Paris's wedding. I had made it abundantly clear to him on numerous occasions how important this event was to me, and he had promised to be my plus-one.

I should have known better.

My skin looked quite pale in the mirror as I stood there, brushing my teeth over the sink while trying to snap out of my bad mood. I made a mental note to squeeze-in a spray-tan at the spa before the wedding, although it'd have to be later on that day after my hair and makeup clients. I rinsed my mouth and stepped into the shower, welcoming the water to cleanse my skin as though I were washing Nick out of my life.

I decided to go with a natural makeup look for my job at the Lavender Dreams Spa, opting for neutral shades on my eyes, lips, and cheeks. Being forced to be a bridesmaid without a date had put me in a sour mood. But as I stared at the nude lipstick in my hand, memories of Nick chastising me popped into my mind.

All that gunk makes you look like a prostitute.

I chucked my nude makeup aside and chose a neon-pink blush and matching lipstick, and then brought it all home with a smoky eyeshadow. It would take one hell of a pleasant surprise to snap me out of that mood, but if any of Nick's current girlfriends showed up at the spa again, maybe they'd gossip to him about me. And knowing that his face would grimace at the thought of my "looking like a prostitute," put a little more pep in my step.

While sliding into a pair of skinny jeans, a white blouse, and short-sleeved tan blazer, I once again considered backing out of the wedding altogether. The weight would be lifted off of my shoulders if I simply called Paris and said, "I'm so sorry, but I can't be in your wedding after all. I'm afraid I contracted a stomach virus from one of my clients."

But that simply wasn't an option when you were a bridesmaid.

I cursed my unlucky stars while brewing some coffee to go, wishing I had never agreed to be in her stupid wedding anyway. The thought of being a bridesmaid without a date was mortifying, but it was too late to find a partner. Anyone I met on such short notice wouldn't have enough time to be adequately vetted, and as much as I wanted to bring someone, I couldn't allow myself to settle for just any guy.

By the time I made it into work, I was fuming.

I pushed through the glass doors painted with intricate lavender flowers and forced a smile at the receptionists sitting behind the large pink-and-purple marble desk. A few clients were waiting for their appointments in the lobby off to the right, fitted with large crushed-velvet couches, Victorian-style end tables full of bouquets, and a built-in waterfall that streamed down the wall—it was all very Zen. One of them helped herself to a cup of herbal tea while eating one of the baked goods Guadalupe had brought in that day. Knowing her, she had probably made the pastries herself.

The spa's tranquility was starting to ease my stress, especially as I stopped to peer out the floor-to-ceiling windows that overlooked the ocean. I may have to attend this wedding without a date, but I got to work and live in paradise.

"There's my favorite girl!"

Guadalupe's warm, motherly voice filled my office as I turned around to see her standing in the doorway, holding a cup of Cuban coffee in one hand and a coconut pastry in the other. Ever since I had started here almost a year ago, she had treated me as though I were her daughter instead of her employee.

Which was fine by me. Between her inability to have children and my being so far away from home, it was a win-win for both of us.

My eyes lit up as the smell of coconut came closer. "If you keep feeding me these pastries, then I might not fit into my bridesmaid dress!"

Guadalupe set the coffee and pastry onto my desk before wrapping her arms around me.

I often counted my blessings that I got to work for Guadalupe. The cosmetology industry was full of catty, bitchy women who hated each other for one reason or another. One girl I had graduated with from cosmetology school went into business with a woman who stole all of her clients, and I'd heard nightmares about some salon owners treating their employees like garbage.

But Guadalupe was one of the sweetest women I had ever met.

"What are you worried about, my dear? Men love women with a thick, curvy body! Especially when they're alto, oscuro y guapo!"

She sat down on the white couch with lavender-colored pillows opposite from my desk, and I sank my teeth into her delicious Cuban pastry. The flaky, buttery texture was exactly what I needed to put me in a good mood for the rest of the day. And her robust Cuban coffee was more potent than anything I could make at home.

"Well, I'll be on the lookout for any tall, dark, and handsome men at Paris's wedding."

Guadalupe's face didn't hide her shock. "What are you talking about, love? Aren't you taking Nick, or has that bastard ghosted you again?"

Hearing her call him a bastard put another smile on my face. "I'm afraid he's ended it for good this time, Guadalupe." I turned around in my seat to make sure I didn't have any more pictures of him in my office.

"That's awful, Margo! You're supposed to be a bridesmaid! How can a bridesmaid go to a wedding without an escort?"

I simply nodded while devouring the rest of my pastry and washing it down with coffee.

Please don't remind me.

"The worst part was, he sent me a text message to end it. The jerk couldn't even do it face to face like a real man."

Guadalupe simply nodded as her body tensed. "Let me tell you something, dear. Nick was never good enough for you. I saw evil in his eyes when we met, but he seemed to make you happy, so I stayed quiet. A real man doesn't waste your time, either."

I thought about other times when Nick had treated me like shit. On more than one occasion, he had blatantly flirted with waitresses while we were placing our order. And they'd flirt right back. In fact, the more I looked back on our dates, I realized that I had never gone home without feeling insecure. And whenever I'd mention it to him, he'd turn it around on me, saying that I was being needy and lacked self-confidence.

Guadalupe was right, and deep down, I knew she had never liked him. Then again, mothers always knew when a man wasn't good enough for their daughters. And as much as I loved my mother, I kind of wished Guadalupe he had been my real one. She reached out and held my hand, using her fingers to rub mine.

"Thank you. I appreciate that. It should still be a fun time, though."

Guadalupe cocked her head at me and raised a perfectly arched brow while leaning back onto the couch. "You're not thinking of canceling, are you?" Nothing got past her.

"If I weren't a member of the bridal party, then yes, I would back out. It'll just be so embarrassing to be the only one at the wedding without a date. And the more I think about it, Guadalupe, the more I think that I will cancel. But please don't say anything if I do, though."

She straightened her petite frame as she stood and put her hands on her hips, staring at me in a motherly fashion. "Now you listen to me, Margo. There are worse things in this world than showing up to a wedding without a date. You are far too young and beautiful to let this bring you down. Look at it as a blessing! Remember how Nick used to flirt with other women in front of you, at your job no less?"

My eyes narrowed as a knot formed in my stomach, remembering that I'd caught Nick being a little too talkative with a temporary receptionist and some clients in the waiting room. He'd seen me standing there and just smiled, as though he hadn't done anything wrong.

I cringed at the memory. "Of course I do, Guadalupe."

"Now just think about how he'd act at a wedding after a few drinks. You'd probably end up being his babysitter. So no, I won't tell anyone about you canceling because you're not going to. Have I made myself clear?"

Both of us giggled at the same moment, and I nodded. Guadalupe kissed me on the cheek and walked back out into the spa, which she owned with her husband, Yuslan. I had loved her as a mother after my very first interview and told myself that even if they didn't hire me, I'd definitely become a customer at Lavender Dreams Spa.

I went to get another coconut pastry and cup of her delicious Cuban coffee and paused a few feet short of my office on the way back. At the end of a long hallway full of massage rooms, clients chose which oil they wanted the massage therapist to use on their skin. The client in the room next to mine had gone with lavender, my favorite scent. It wafted under the sturdy door and into the hallway. I stood there for several minutes with my eyes shut, inhaling deeply, and appreciating the calming, floral aroma until another door opened.

"Good morning," I said to a woman who had paused there in a plush, terrycloth robe.

She seemed concerned about why I was just standing in the hall with my eyes closed, but I wasn't about to tell her. Instead, I smiled and went into my office and closed the door.

When I had started at the spa, I had never expected to have an office. The other salons I had applied to had a casual setup where clients checked in with the receptionist, and you were lucky if you found a seat at the break room table.

But not at Lavender Dreams Spa.

My office was nearly the size of my bedroom and provided me with stunning views of the shore. Once the door was closed, it was almost impossible to hear anything in the hallway, and I often used the time between clients to write in my journal or read a book.

According to my schedule for the next few days, I had three more clients than I did last month.

Thank God.

Their treatments included everything from basic haircuts to coloring, along with a few extension requests. It was so fulfilling to sit a client down in the chair and transform their hair into something completely different. My favorite treatment was changing someone's hair color to an entirely different shade and then seeing their face light up in the mirror.

Thankfully, nobody had complained about the final results yet.

My first client wasn't until ten o'clock that morning, which gave me some time to relax and get ready. I fought every urge to look at Nick's social media accounts during that time, too. Guadalupe was right about him. He had a wandering eye, and there were several instances where I had questioned his faithfulness.

Even though I was still livid that he had dumped me right before the wedding, I had started to see it from Guadalupe's point of view. Once Nick began drinking, he became a party boy without limitations or a filter. He would have flirted with other women at the wedding, and that would have made me look like a fool.

It still sucked that I wouldn't have a date, though.

Remembering that I wanted to get tanned before the wedding, I quickly scheduled an appointment later on that day after all of my clients. Maybe I'd end up meeting someone Guadalupe would approve of, but of course, he'd have to be *alto, oscuro y guapo* to measure up to her standards.

2

Chase

The gorgeous blue sky in Key Biscayne, Florida, welcomed me home as the airplane pilot announced that we'd be landing shortly. I hadn't planned on spending so much time in San Francisco, but the proffered deal for my latest round of cellphone software was too good to pass up. It was a profitable exchange that would only serve to expand my business ventures in the technology world.

The only downside to a successful business trip was an unsuccessful social life. Coming home to an empty place did bring me down a little bit, even when I tried not to focus on it.

As I looked down into the ocean, a few sharks swam far

away from the shore while people sunbathed. The scenery was one of the many reasons I chose to call Key Biscayne my home. It would have been nicer to know that I was returning home to a woman waiting for me, but I couldn't have been more single.

After grabbing a bottle of water from my carry-on bag, I tackled the massive pile of emails demanding my attention.

I knocked out the first group regarding my company's laptops, which had consistently been the number-one selling brand for several years. Competitors simply didn't stand a chance against the models we put out, which featured cutting-edge technology and software nearly impossible to hack, and it was all exclusive to our brand.

After replying to those that warranted a response and forwarding the others for someone else to handle, I moved to the next batch. My televisions line was the second bestseller on the market. And while I couldn't stand that we weren't number one, I was still proud of that position. The amount of time and effort that my team and I had put into creating that technology should have yielded us the number-one spot, but it gave us something to strive for.

But it was my home security products that took up the bulk of my email and gave me notoriety around Key Biscayne. Most of the people I knew had it installed in both their homes, vacation properties, and businesses. One of my neighbors had even contacted me while I was out in San Francisco, thanking me because it had helped to stop an intruder from getting too far onto his property.

That's what I loved most about what I did for a living. Even though I was a billionaire and could practically swim in all of the money I had earned, knowing that people truly enjoyed and benefited from my products satisfied me. And I took pride in staying hands-on with the technology and its creation.

As we got closer to landing, I wondered if I would ever feel the satisfaction I did in my career in my personal life. I loved going to work, and I wanted to love coming home. People would do just about anything to have my life between my luxury sports cars and trips around the world, but I always dreaded returning. To me, it was nothing more than a big house, because a home had a wife, kids—a family. I didn't even have a dog.

When I was first looking for a place to live in Key Biscayne, I knew I wanted a Spanish-style mansion—a place that had charm and lots of character. But I soon discovered that all of the beautiful crown molding and fancy, handmade tile in the world didn't make for a happy life, just a stunning home.

Having people waiting for your return made you happy.

I had tried discussing my thoughts with some of my friends, but they just shrugged it off. The theory—regardless of its validity—being that it wasn't masculine to want someone to share your life with, and the only reason men got married and had kids was to maintain a certain image. I lived in a social circle where if you wanted to be a successful businessman, then it was true, you needed to come off as every bit of a family man when you reached a certain age. Especially if you wanted to become a politician.

I never saw myself in politics, but after my last serious relationship, I was starting to hate being alone all of the time. Sleeping alone wasn't all that it was cracked up to be; that was for damn sure.

My cellphone started to ring right as I was putting it away.

Why do people call when they can just send a text message?

When I saw that it was my sister, Ginger, I understood why she called. "Hey, Ginger. I'm getting ready to land in Key Biscayne. What's going on?"

Without so much as a hello, she launched into the reason for her call. "You didn't forget about Paris's wedding, right? Because it's coming up, and she's expecting both of us to be there. I know you're this big tech titan with all of these companies, and you're always on the go, but you *need* to be there with me."

I often thought about sending my assistant in Ginger's place and replacing her coffee with decaf. "Of course I didn't forget! I'm looking forward to going, Ginger. Besides, I can't wait to see this guy you're bringing."

"Oh my gosh, you are going to *love* Anthony! He is such a sweetheart."

He could be the greatest guy in the world; it didn't mean he was good enough for my sister. "How would I know? You two have been together for a while, and I have yet to meet him."

I could feel her eyes rolling at me through the phone.

"Anthony's just shy, Chase. Why are you always so judgmental about my boyfriends?"

I had been round and round with my sister about this, but apparently, it bore repeating. "I'm judgmental about them because I'm a guy, Ginger, and I know what guys are like. I just don't want to see you be strung along by someone who's not worth your time, that's all."

"And what makes you assume that he's stringing me along? Just because he hasn't found the time to meet anyone in the family?"

"Yup." That pretty much summed it up. If my sister were important to this loser, then he'd get with the program and introduce himself—that's what men did who intended to keep a woman. They embedded themselves into that girl's life.

"For the record, big brother, I really think Anthony could be the one." *She* may think it. That didn't mean *he* did, and that right there was my whole issue.

"I'll be the judge of that, Ginger. You've said this about other guys, too, you know? As a guy, I can tell from a mile away when another one is stringing a woman along. Maybe I'm wrong, but if I were really into someone, I would have met their family by now." I didn't beeline for a woman's parents, but if I were serious about her, I wanted to know what came along with her. If I couldn't tolerate her family or saw some red flag, I needed to find out sooner rather than later.

She huffed on the other end. "By the time this wedding is over, Chase, you're going to be apologizing to both Anthony and me for not even giving him a chance. I look forward to that moment too."

I laughed while shaking my head—not that she could see me—and at that same moment, my best friend beeped in.

"I gotta go. Jorge is calling on the other line, and we're about to land. Later."

I clicked over to him before Ginger could say another word. After a long flight back from San Francisco, I wasn't in the mood to deal with her drama.

"Chase! Welcome back from Cali, my man. How was your trip?"

"Eh, it was all right. Nothing but business meetings, though, so definitely not a vacation. Are you looking forward to Paris's wedding?"

"I purchased a new Armani suit today, Chase. I can't wait to meet some hot bridesmaids."

"Well, Paris is pretty attractive, so I'm sure her friends are too. Aren't you bringing a date, though?"

Jorge laughed into the phone so hard that I was sure people seated around me heard him. "Hell no! Are you?"

"Nope." It might have been a tad messed up but knowing that I wouldn't be the only dateless man made me feel a hell of a lot better.

"Good, that means we get a chance at hooking up with some of those bridesmaids. I'm hoping there's a sexy blonde there, or maybe a redhead. I haven't slept with a redhead yet."

The way Jorge spoke about women made my stomach do flips. He was more of a "bro" type than me, although he did have some good qualities. I kept telling myself that he'd change once he found "the one," but it didn't really matter either way.

"I don't know about that, Jorge."

"Oh, come on, man. They expect guys like us to show up eligible. We'll have all of the hot women at the reception lining up to talk with us, hoping we'll choose them to bring them back to a hotel room. You know how weddings go."

"No, no, I don't." I chuckled at his attitude, but only because we'd had this discussion more times than I could count, and neither of us ever changed. "And I don't buy that comment about us needing to be eligible. It's not a bachelor auction."

"You're too uptight, Chase." Jorge was the exact opposite of that, which was what made us such great friends. "Do you know what you need?" He was going to tell me, so I just waited. "A vacation that doesn't include any type of business. Just you, me, and some fine-ass women to fool around with. We should set something up after this wedding. What do you say?"

"I'm gonna have to pass, Jorge. That's not really my scene. The wedding should be fun, though. Anyway, I gotta get going."

If the two of us had been in a restaurant, I would have made him shut-up the second he began discussing women as though they were objects.

"Why are you in such a rush?"

The "fasten your seatbelts" light came on, and several other passengers were glaring at me.

"The plane is about to land, so I gotta put my phone away. I'll call you later on tonight, though, all right?"

"Yeah, later, man."

Jorge hung up before I could hit the end button. I didn't mean to offend him, but this idea that men like us were expected to be bachelors was nothing short of nauseating. I didn't want to lead a life alone, and I sure didn't want to wake up next to Jorge—ever.

I leaned back and closed my eyes the rest of the trip, right up until the plane landed. Flying had never bothered me that much. I was much more afraid of getting into a car accident than a plane crash, but knowing that my home would be empty had left me melancholy. I didn't want to admit it out loud, but I hated being this lonely.

As the plane lowered and hit the tarmac, I pictured opening up the front doors to my Spanish-style mansion and it being so quiet that I could hear a pin drop. It happened every time I returned from one of my business trips, or hell, from anywhere. My maid had probably left me a vase full of flowers on the mantle, just as she always did, but it wasn't the same as having someone with their arms open, waiting for you.

The pilot announced that we could get off the plane, yet I remained seated for several minutes. It wasn't until the flight attendant smiled at me that I finally stood.

"Sorry, guess I'm just a little tired. Thank you for a pleasant flight."

Everyone around me was rushing to grab their luggage, whereas I was moving at a snail's pace. It wasn't until my driver waved at me that my feet moved faster.

Our eyes met in the rearview mirror once he adjusted it. "Where to, sir?"

"Um, would you mind driving me around for a little bit? I have some work stuff to do on my phone." The truth was, I just wasn't ready to step into isolation.

"Of course."

Instead of work emails, however, I went to my ex-girlfriend's Instagram page. There was Amber, on her honeymoon with her high school sweetheart, Bradley. The two of them looked so happy on the beach in Hawaii. She was wearing a short, white sundress with bright-red flowers in her hair. Bradley had his arms wrapped around her, and I zoomed in on the size of her engagement ring.

Bradley was also quite wealthy.

I powered off my phone and chucked it into my briefcase, remembering all of the fun we'd had together. Amber had been my first true love, and all I did was screw it up. My mind was obsessed with nothing but money, power, and prestige—success at any cost. Even when I became a millionaire, it still wasn't enough.

I always wanted more.

The pit in my stomach seemed to get bigger as I realized that I was about to walk into an empty house, while Amber was celebrating the most significant moment of her life —without me.

That should be us on that beach, with my ring on her finger and my arms around her waist.

I kept running my hands through my hair, hoping it'd snap me back to reality, but it didn't work.

"Can you take me to Cabana Lust? I need a drink."

"Of course, sir."

My driver patiently waited in the limo as I sat down at the outside bar.

The bartender was pretty sexy and tried flirting with me, but all I could think about was Amber. She smiled at me and asked, "What'll it be, sweetheart?"

"Between the Sheets." I hated the name—it sounded like it would come with a pink umbrella—but I loved the taste of citrus, triple sec, and rum.

As I sipped the mixed drink, music started playing, and I was instantly transported back to my memories with my now-married ex. I had completely ruined our relationship, and even when Amber had ended things, I couldn't blame her. I was never there for her when she needed me. During those nights, when she was dealing with the death of her mother, I was up late, trying to become a billionaire.

And it had worked—I had added another zero to my bank account and successfully lost the girl.

Yet as I went through two more mixed drinks, I realized that all of the alcohol in the world couldn't distract me from loneliness.

3

Margo

The Miami Beach sun wasn't the only thing waking me up that morning.

As my eyes squinted through the window, my phone started to go off with an incoming call. There were only a few people who called instead of texting me, and I didn't even have to look at the caller ID to know who it was so early in the morning.

"Good morning, Ginger."

"Oh my gosh, my life is completely over!"

"What happened now?" I forced myself out of bed and into the kitchen, where I kept Ginger on speakerphone while preparing some coffee.

"Anthony dumped me! And of all the times to break-up

with me, he did it the morning of the wedding! I cannot go to this thing without a date, Margo. Do you understand? I cannot!"

The coffee dripped a little too slowly into my mug, which said the American Academy of Cosmetology. One of my favorite teachers had given it to me as a graduation gift, and I drank coffee from it every morning.

"If he broke up with you when you needed him the most, then you're better off without him, Ginger. I know it's hard, believe me, but it's probably for the best."

Her sobbing intensified as I spoke, and even though she had a tendency to be a drama queen, she was still my best friend. I did feel bad for her.

"I've been dumped before so that part is water under the bridge, but going to this wedding without a date is simply not an option, Margo. I refuse to go without a date!"

"Look, I know it's tough right now, but I promise you that being single isn't the end of the world." I wasn't sure where any of this was coming from since just yesterday I was complaining about the same things, but sometimes as a friend, you have to fake it until you make it. "I'm single, too, you know. Why don't we go together?"

"Are you kidding me, Margo? I'd rather die than show up without a guy!"

"Hey! I resent that comment. I'm showing up alone, and there's no shame in that."

"Well, that's you, Margo. You and I are just different. You don't care that hundreds of people will be looking at you in a bridesmaid dress, watching everyone dance with their date as you casually sip champagne. But I do care what people think about me." She had taken melodramatic to a whole new level —this wedding wasn't about *her*. And it was unlikely that anyone cared if either of us showed up with a date or each other.

I swallowed a big sip of coffee before defending myself. "Are you saying that I'm going to look like a fool at this wedding, Ginger? Are you suggesting that I'm going to be one big joke because I won't be on a man's arm? Because if you are, that's pretty messed up." I realized the truth in my words as they came out.

Ginger let out a sigh. "Look, as I said, you and I are different. Besides, you're gorgeous, and I'm sure some guy will want to get to know you, so it's not as though you'll be single for long."

"You're just as pretty, Ginger!"

"You still don't get it, do you? People will be looking at me as I walk around without a date. That's humiliating! And the worst part is that Chase kept hinting that Anthony was stringing me along. I hate when he's right!"

She and her brother had a love-hate relationship. They were super close, but she despised that Chase could always see her life from a different perspective than she could—and that he was always right. I'd never met the guy—he was always jetting somewhere to show off a TV or phone or something—but I'd heard Ginger talk about him enough to know that she should listen to him.

"Look, both of us have to go to this wedding. Paris is one of our closest friends. So date or no date, you and I are in this together—without men. Don't you even think about canceling on me, either. I'm counting on you to be my plus-one."

Ginger was slamming something around on the other end of the phone, but I had no idea what it was. "Maybe I can hit up some old boyfriend from high school on social media and see if they're available today. Who wouldn't turn down a free meal and an open bar?"

"Ginger, don't you dare do that! There's a reason they're not in your life anymore. You're too dramatic. Why don't you just come over here so we can work out this whole situation?"

She was silent for a few minutes as I waited for an answer. "Fine, I'll be over there in an hour or so. But don't be surprised if I find a date before the wedding this afternoon!"

Out of all of my friends, Ginger could have won an Oscar for her dramatic performances.

I spent the next hour tidying up my apartment and consuming more coffee, although it didn't taste nearly as good as Guadalupe's Cuban blend. I kept replaying scenarios in my mind about what would happen when people saw me without a date. After hearing Ginger's reaction to being dateless, I accepted that I needed to get a grip. Nobody cared who I was there—or not there—with. They were coming to see Paris and John, not Ginger or me.

I also kept thinking about what Guadalupe had said to me at the salon, and she was right about Nick. If anything, I had dodged a bullet by not having him come with me to the wedding. Since I was someone who cared what people thought of me, then shouldn't I be thankful that the loser dumped me and save me the embarrassment of being stuck babysitting a grown-ass man?

It still would have been nice to bring someone to the wedding, though. I always enjoyed dancing, and Paris and John had hired a live band.

Maybe someone will feel bad and let me take a spin with their date.

If no guy wanted to dance, then I wasn't above pulling a group of bridesmaids out onto the floor. One way or another, I would have a good time.

I poured myself another cup of coffee, mainly because I knew Ginger would be arriving any second, and she tended to talk a mile a minute. I was a bit rougher with her on the phone than I should have been, but the woman seriously needed to get a grip. When I was devastated about not having a date, I didn't sound the alarm for World War III—at least not to Ginger. I silently panicked in my head, and then Guadalupe quickly shut down any thought of bailing on Paris, which ended my freakout...*for the most part.*

As I was about to make my bed, Ginger texted me that she had arrived and would be up shortly. I unlocked the front door and went back to my bed, only to jump in the air a minute later.

"I found a date, Margo! I actually have a date!" Ginger

came running into my bedroom, where she wrapped her arms around me a little too enthusiastically.

"First of all, I haven't had enough coffee to deal with that level of excitement, so let's tone it down a notch. And second of all, how did you find someone so quickly?"

Ginger sat on the edge of my bed, looking as excited as a little girl who just got a pony for her birthday. "Chase is going to be my date!"

If there were ever a time to bite my tongue, it was right at that moment. "You're...going to the wedding...with your *brother*? As your plus-one?"

Ginger's head leaned back a bit. "Yes, but why do you sound so taken aback?"

"Oh no, I'm not taken aback! I'm just surprised that you found a date for the wedding so quickly, that's all." Although I wasn't sure taking her brother would look any better than going solo.

She waved her hand in front of her face, insinuating that it was no big deal. "Oh, please. Chase and I have always been close, and he's going to the wedding anyway. It just makes sense that we go together!"

I merely nodded while making the rest of my bed, thereby forcing Ginger to stand up and walk over to the window.

"I'm an only child, so forgive me for being a little surprised by this new...arrangement. I never had a sister, let alone a brother."

I would rather die than have my brother be my date. That was as bad as having your mom arrange for your cousin to take you to the prom—nope!

"You have no idea what you missed out on, Margo! Chase has always been there for me, and today is no exception. When I told him that Anthony dumped me, he was pissed, saying he was right. Anyway, I held that over his head as a reason to accompany me."

As I fluffed my pillows, I realized that being a dateless bridesmaid wasn't so bad. I'd rather go alone than with a sibling...or a cousin. "Well, as you said, the two of us are quite different, and I don't mind going solo."

Ginger's arm wrapped around my waist as she leaned her head on my shoulder. "Oh, you poor thing! I wish I knew someone who could take you, but I've already snagged my brother!"

"Believe me, it's not a problem. Now, we should probably start getting ready for the wedding. Have you showered yet?"

We spent the rest of the morning getting ready for the wedding since Ginger had brought her bridesmaid dress over with her. In between showering, we gossiped about some of the people who would be at the wedding, discussed how the dinners didn't seem too filling, and how we were thrilled about having an open bar.

"That should cheer you up," Ginger said while deciding on a shade of lipstick.

"Are you suggesting that I get drunk to forget that I don't have a date?"

"Why not? That's what I would do, you know, if my brother hadn't saved me."

If I had to go with my brother to a wedding, I'd drink myself into a coma.

I ignored her comment and focused on my makeup. "I can't decide between these two lipstick shades. Which one do you like?"

Ginger looked at both shades, which were merely different hues of nude, and pointed to the darker one. "Your skin is a little pale, and that should liven it up a bit."

I marched over to my full-length mirror, where I looked at myself from head to toe. "I had Vanessa give me one of those spray-tans where they massage it into your skin. I'm not that pale."

Ginger held her arm up to mine, which was a little bit darker, and smiled. "You're not as dark as me."

At least I'm not going on a date with my brother.

BY LATE AFTERNOON, THE TWO OF US WERE MORE THAN ready to go to Paris's wedding. Since Ginger would be going with Chase, they offered to have me ride with them to the ceremony and then the reception.

"Oh, he's here! Chase just texted me!"

You shouldn't be this excited about seeing your brother—whom you're dating.

I grabbed my bag as the two of us went to the front door,

opening it just in time to see Chase standing on the other side. It had been a long time since I had felt weak in the knees, and at that moment, I struggled to balance myself in my high heels. Chase and I locked eyes for several intense seconds, and all I could do was muster a barely audible "hello."

He was standing there in a Gucci suit and chocolate-colored tie, which matched perfectly with his eyes. His hair was slicked back, but not in a gross, crusty way like he'd used too much gel. Chase just knew how to style his hair, and I so desperately wanted to run my hands through it.

"It's a pleasure to meet you, Margo."

Ginger glared at him and then me, before obnoxiously clearing her throat. "Shall we leave, or are we just going to stand out here in the hallway and gawk?"

I ignored Ginger's attitude while continuing to stare at Chase. He could have been straight out of a fashion magazine the way his muscles stood out underneath his clothes and his perfect, bright-white teeth accentuated his smile that was directed right at me.

"Are you ladies ready to get into the limousine?"

Once again, Ginger cleared her throat, which finally snapped me back to reality. "Did you say limo? You rented a limo?"

"I didn't rent it, but yes, there is one waiting," he said while chuckling. "It'll take us to both the wedding and the reception. And it prevents any of us from having to drive home tonight."

Ginger slid her arm through her brother's while gazing into his eyes. "See, Margo! I told you how wonderful my brother is."

I smirked while locking the door behind me. "That's funny. I thought limos were only for the bride and groom."

Ginger gave me another dirty look as we turned to leave, but not before I caught Chase grinning at me.

This wedding might not be so bad, after all.

4

Chase

The ceremony was, of course, over the top and beautiful. Paris and her new husband, John, were every bit the perfect couple. He towered over her at just under six -feet, five-inches, whereas she was a little over five-feet. They got married in the church John had attended since he was a child. In fact, he was baptized into Catholicism just a few feet away from where they recited their vows. As the two of them kissed, everyone clapped, and there was only one dry set of eyes in the audience.

Mine.

I couldn't take my eyes off of Margo throughout the ceremony. Since she was a bridesmaid, anyone looking at me would assume that I was staring at Paris and John. But from the moment Margo took her place at the altar, she was the only thing I was interested in.

Margo was the most beautiful woman I had ever seen. Her long, light-brown hair was styled in layers that casually framed her heart-shaped face, and her piercing blue eyes were the same color as the pristine, crystal-blue waters of Miami Beach. From the moment our eyes had locked, time and space stood still. Neither one of us had been able to say more than a few words to each other, but there was no denying the instant chemistry.

That was until Ginger spoke up, of course.

After the ceremony, Ginger, Margo, and I climbed into the limo and headed for the reception. I tried to talk to Margo during the ride over there, but Ginger simply would not shut up. She kept chatting a mile a minute about how beautiful it was to see her best friends get married. Judging by the look on Margo's face, she also wanted Ginger to zip it for a bit. It was going to be a long evening, and it was far too early for me to pop some pain pills for a mounting headache.

When we got to the reception, the photographer wanted to take more pictures of the wedding party. All we could do was wait, and I had tried my best to sit next to Margo while doing so. But Ginger noticed me and squeezed herself between us, even digging my side with her elbow. It was the same elbow dig that she had given me in the limo, and every time she had caught me staring at Margo.

You're my sister! Why are you getting jealous?

Margo kept straightening her dress while we waited for

the photographer, making sure that it wasn't crinkling up or getting caught underneath the chair.

I thought it looked perfect. "That dress is amazing, Margo. It looks fantastic on you."

Her cheeks blushed as she leaned back, deciding that she didn't need to fidget with her clothes. "Well, thank you, Chase."

"Ahem," Ginger shouted, causing everyone, including the photographer, to turn around.

My obnoxious, bratty, younger sister aside, the whole day was turning out to be much more fun than I had anticipated. And seeing Margo in that stunning dress was just the icing on the cake. I wasn't current with fashion trends, but I knew it was a rose gold mermaid-style dress with exceptionally low cleavage. The low-cut surprised me since most brides didn't want any attention taken away from them on their big day.

But then again, Paris's dress was also low-cut, so they complemented each other.

I'm sure John enjoyed that view.

Margo's matching rose gold heels popped out as she reached into her purse, where I watched her touch-up her makeup. She used rice paper to blot away any excess oil from her soft skin, then dabbed a little bit of blush onto her cheekbones. I was about to tell her not to bother, that she looked stunning, but once again, Ginger caught me staring and elbowed my side.

"Ow! What is your problem, Ginger?"

My sister glared at me and then Margo as if silently telling her to back away.

I'm your brother, and this is so weird.

The photographer finally turned to Ginger and Margo. "All right, why don't the bridesmaids join the couple?"

My jaw nearly hit the floor as I watched Margo walk over, giving me a good glimpse of her gorgeous backside. I shifted in my seat a bit, suddenly aware that I was getting a bit too aroused at a wedding reception.

After taking photographs, all of the guests started to file in, and the reception was finally taking off. Everywhere Margo went, my eyes followed—to the bathroom, for more champagne, and even when she went to mingle with other guests. It was hard to do so under the watchful eye of my jealous sibling, but there was something about Margo that I was becoming obsessed with.

Ginger kicked my leg from underneath the table. "I want to dance, Chase. Now."

I was about to protest, telling her that we should probably dance with other people we aren't, you know, related to, but there was no getting through to her. She grabbed my hand and yanked me out onto the dance floor, where the live band began playing a slow song. I encouraged Ginger to rest her head on my shoulder, just so she wouldn't see me looking at Margo.

It worked. But it was also a little strange.

Margo was off to the side, eating an appetizer and sipping champagne while casually looking over at us. And every time she did, I smiled directly at her. By the time the song was about halfway through, I was ready to spin Ginger off to someone else and ask Margo to dance. So, I eyed the crowd to find an eligible bachelor. As much as I wanted to get rid of Ginger, I didn't want just anyone dancing with my little sister.

The only one without a date, though, was Jorge.

Crap.

I slowly made our way over to Jorge, who was leaning up against the wall and surveying the crowd. Looking for a redhead, no doubt—or maybe a blonde. He wasn't my first choice when it came to having another man touch my sister, given his history with women, but there was no other choice. It was him, or I'd be forced to dance with Ginger all night, leaving Margo up for grabs with other men.

And just knowing that Jorge might flirt with her sealed the deal for me.

Ginger was going to dance with Jorge.

As he and I made eye contact, I nodded to come over, and he promptly did. The way he walked toward me in his new, expensive suit, adjusting his tie while ogling other ladies along the way, made me want to vomit. I couldn't believe I was about to hand off my sister to him.

"Jorge, you remember my younger sister, Ginger, right?"

He eyed her up and down like a piece of meat; that did not sit well with me. I glared at him, hoping he'd catch my gaze, but he was too focused on sizing up my sister.

"Of course, I do! It's so nice to see you again, Ginger. That was quite a wedding ceremony, wasn't it?"

Ginger didn't look too happy about the sudden switch. "Uh-huh."

She extended her hand to Jorge, and he immediately put it to his lips, kissing it while glancing in my direction. His kiss still didn't warm her up to the idea of dancing with him, though.

"If you don't mind, Ginger, I'm going to pass you off to Jorge for a bit. And don't worry, he's a terrific dancer. Aren't you, Jorge?"

He made a cheesy dance move, which caught the attention of several other people. And not in the right way.

As I slid between the two of them, making my way toward Margo, I whispered into Jorge's ear, and chuckled, "If you do anything to hurt my little sister, the police will never find your body."

Jorge smirked before slowly taking Ginger's hand and leading her onto the dance floor. I waited long enough to make sure he didn't put his hands on her ass. And Jorge proved to be a gentleman, at least, while I was watching.

Margo was ordering a drink at the bar, so that's where I jetted off to, forcing my way between other people as I went. A few of them gave me dirty looks, but I just brushed it off. I never backed down from getting what I wanted, especially when it came to women.

"Can I get another glass of champagne?"

The bartender nodded at Margo while pouring her a glass, then turned his attention to me. "And what can I get you, sir?"

"Beer on tap, please."

Margo turned and smiled, and once again, I found it hard to speak. Being this close to her gave me a better view of those long, thick eyelashes and soft skin. I fought every urge to run my fingers along her cheeks to feel the touch of a woman's skin with my hand. It had been too long since I'd been with anyone.

"We haven't properly met, but I'm Chase, and you're best friends with my younger sister, Ginger, who's acting like an odd duck tonight."

Margo giggled while shaking my extended hand. "It's a pleasure to meet you, Chase. And yes, I'm Margo, your younger sister's best friend."

It didn't escape my attention that she didn't comment on Ginger's behavior.

We sipped our drinks for an awkward few seconds, occasionally looking out at the dance floor before I was finally able to make some small talk.

"That wedding was beautiful, wasn't it?"

Margo nodded while sipping her champagne. "It was amazing. Very typical of John and Paris. They're classy people."

I leaned on the glass bar a little bit, trying to make myself appear casual while dealing with a stomach full of butterflies. "Well, you seem pretty classy yourself. The way you handled yourself during the ceremony, and that dress perfectly complements your body. You carry yourself with a tremendous amount of grace."

"Thank you very much." Margo blushed just a hint at my

compliments. "I was worried that I'd trip while walking down the aisle. These heels are pretty high." She held her leg out to show me, but I wanted to peek up a bit higher along her slender leg instead. Thankfully I kept my gaze on her shoes.

"That's probably why men don't wear heels. We'd fall flat on our faces. Seriously, I give you ladies a lot of credit for going through what you do for fashion."

"It's not always easy. Sometimes when my boss isn't looking, I slide out of my heels. It's painful to stand in them all day."

I chuckled a little bit, picturing her running around the spa barefoot.

"Well, if I ever come into your spa, then I'll be sure to do a double-take at your feet."

"Have you ever been to a spa before, Chase?"

I suddenly pictured her standing over me, massaging my back as her breasts dropped dangerously close to my body. "Um, yes," I said, shaking myself out of that little trance. "It's been a while, though. In fact, I had shoulder surgery and should probably make an appointment for a massage sometime."

"Ahem."

Margo and I turned around to find Ginger staring at us, once again with her arms folded.

"Jorge was boring. Chase, order me a glass of chardonnay. But not the dry kind. I hate dry wine."

I turned around to face the bartender while rolling my

eyes, and he gave me a knowing smile. "My *sister* will have a glass of chardonnay, but nothing dry. Whatever that means."

Ginger started to describe the taste of dry wine, but thankfully Margo interjected when the band began to play a new song.

"Oh, I love this song! Ginger, this is my favorite song."

I nearly dropped my glass of beer, while Ginger, on the other hand, looked utterly pissed off. "Would you like to dance, Margo?"

I held out my hand, and she took it, and even though I felt Ginger staring into my back as we walked onto the dance floor, I just didn't care. I was finally getting a chance to dance with Margo, to press my body up against hers in that gorgeous, tight-fitting dress with a low-cut neckline. To be even closer to her intoxicating scent, which reminded me of lavender and coconuts.

As I twirled her around a few times, I glanced over at Ginger, who was sulking at the bar.

Tough luck, sis. Your friend is smoking hot.

5

Margo

Chase was one hell of a good dancer. He casually rolled me out at all the right moments and then seamlessly pulled me back in. His hips felt incredible pressed up against mine, gyrating right along with the song. And I didn't miss the fact that he had pulled me in pretty tight a few times while sneaking a peek down my dress.

That was fine by me, though. I was quite proud of my cleavage.

Thank you, Mom!

Nick had never worn any cologne, so it had been a long time since I had smelled one, but whatever Chase was wearing was getting me aroused. It was musky with notes of amber. I leaned my head on his shoulders a few times to get a bitter whiff of it. It mixed perfectly with his natural, intoxicating, masculine scent. In fact, I would have loved to have buried my face in his neck.

A few members of the wedding party watched us dancing, including some very jealous women. That was their problem. They had brought dates, and this tall, dark, and handsome man was all mine...for the time being. But I knew it wouldn't be long before Ginger threw another temper tantrum about me hogging her date.

Chase was such a good dance partner that the lead singer of the band waved at us, nodding as we waltzed by. His arm gripped my back nice and tight, holding me in place as I struggled to keep up with his moves.

As the band finished the first song and seamlessly moved into the next, Chase turned around so that I was facing the bar again. And that's when I caught Ginger glaring at us, and judging by her posture, she was less than pleased. She could have passed as a toddler on the verge of throwing a fit, all because her date was dancing with someone else—her date who happened to share her DNA. Ginger might have been my best friend, but she desperately needed to grow up. Sure, maybe I was hogging his time, but I honestly didn't think it was that big of a deal.

He's your brother!

Chase twirled me around again, causing me to forget all about his angry sister and forcing me to giggle.

"You are such a good dancer, Chase! Did you receive any formal training?"

His chocolate eyes peered into mine, and once again, my knees went weak. "Not really, although I did accompany Ginger to her senior prom because she couldn't get a date. But don't tell her that I told you. It bruised her ego that her boyfriend dumped her right before the big night."

"Just like Anthony did to her today, right? Poor girl can't catch a break. However, it's generous of you to come as her date tonight. I don't know of any other man who would do that for their...sister. She was so determined not to be in the wedding party without a plus-one."

Chase could read the apprehension in my face and by the tone of my voice. "I know what you're thinking. It's weird for a brother to be his sister's date to a wedding—and prom—but I only did it to be a gentleman. Some women just don't want to be solo. That's all there is to it, I promise."

The band once again seamlessly transitioned into another song, while Chase and I continued dancing. This time he brought us a little too close to where Ginger stood, and I could feel the tension in the air as he swung me around.

Her eyes sent daggers our way, making it abundantly clear that I was ruining her night.

"I don't think Ginger's very happy right now, Chase. Did you see the way she looked at us?"

Chase glanced over at Ginger, and she mouthed something to him, although I couldn't tell what it was. He simply rolled his eyes and shifted his attention back to me.

"Just ignore her. She's a good person, but she hates not being the center of attention."

"Gotcha. I don't have any siblings, so I couldn't exactly ask a brother to accompany me tonight."

His hands dipped a little lower on my hips, stopping short of my ass. I wouldn't have minded it if he gave me a little squeeze.

"It's hard to believe that someone as beautiful as you came here single, Margo. And I hope I'm not too forward, but you're quite breathtaking."

Once again, I couldn't help but blush as I rested my head on his shoulder, grateful that I hadn't bowed out at the last minute. I made a mental note to thank Guadalupe tomorrow.

"Thank you. I was dating a guy, but we just broke up."

Chase pulled back and stared into my eyes. "How could any guy not want to be your date to a wedding?"

We giggled as he twirled me around, and this time, he positioned us so that my back was pressing up against his chest. Chase's hands wrapped around my stomach as I looked up over my shoulder and into his eyes, then turned around to see Ginger with her hands in fists and at her sides.

"As much as I enjoy dancing with you, maybe you should spend the next song with your sister. Look at her. She's about to have a fit."

Ginger continued glaring at both of us, but Chase insisted that we keep on dancing into the next song. This time he dipped me a few times, causing my low-cut dress to drop even more. His hands pressed firmly into my lower back, making sure I didn't fall as he slowly pulled me up. And at no point did Ginger stop giving us the death stare.

We waltzed all across the dance floor, the two of us lost in our own little world as people around us looked on with envy. And how could they not watch Chase dancing? He was so graceful, elegant, but also masculine, and I just knew that Nick would never have shown me such a good time if he had ended up coming.

"Ginger's a grown woman who can take care of herself. Besides, I'm sure some guy will see her sulking and offer to dance with her. So, what do you do for a living?"

"I'm a beautician at Lavender Dreams Spa, which is how I met Ginger. The two of us hit it off when I started there a few months ago. What about you? What do you do for a living?" I knew the gist of it, but it was a gateway to conversation.

He shot Ginger a dirty look as she obnoxiously grabbed a chair and sat down, calling unnecessary attention to her dramatic flair.

"I'm in the technology business. Have my own line of laptops, televisions, and home security systems."

In other words, he's loaded.

"That's amazing. You have to be pretty smart to get into that line of work."

Why did I sound so stupid just now?

Thankfully, Chase laughed at my little comment. "Not really. Once you get the basics down, it's pretty easy to build just about any piece of equipment. And yes, it does pay well."

The more he and I chatted while dancing, the more I wanted to get to know him. It wasn't just that he was a successful technology tycoon, although that did help. Chase was easy to chat with and was a fantastic dancer. It would be nice to have someone to go dancing with, seeing as how that had been a favorite hobby of mine since I was a little girl.

My only concern was that he was my best friend's brother. When it came to most female friendships, a woman would be ecstatic to have her best friend date one of her brothers. After all, it gave them hope that one day they'd become sisters-in-law.

But not Ginger.

As another song started to play, both of us looked over at Ginger, who was now tapping her feet and nails so vigorously that I could imagine I heard them over the band playing. If I wanted to see Chase after the reception, we would have to be watchful of his jealous sister.

It was hard to believe that Chase and I hadn't stopped dancing for four songs, and if I had my way, we would have kept right on going. I wanted to dance with him until it was time to go home, just the two of us on the floor as all of the other couples grew tired. The band would keep on playing as we got to know each other, pressing our bodies up against each other while occasionally looking over at Ginger pouting.

But she put a stop to that as soon as the band went into song number five.

Ginger marched right over, her petite feet stomping on the pink-marble floor along the way, before stopping directly in front of us. Chase and I were standing in the center of the dance floor, as though we were the focus of the entire event, while couples danced all around us.

"If you don't mind, Margo, I'd like to have a dance with *my* date." She said it like a jealous girlfriend, and something about it rubbed me wrong.

Instead of causing a scene, I gave Ginger an apologetic smile, then quietly stepped away. But not before looking back at Chase, who watched me with equal sadness in his eyes as I made my way over to my table. All I could do was sit down and pretend to have a good time, faking conversation with people as I watched Ginger dance with a man I so desperately wanted to get to know better.

A few of my friends came over and made small talk, but it was nothing too exciting. Just chit-chat about the Miami heat, politics, and if we really thought that John and Paris would stay married—typical wedding gossip.

"Of course they'll stay married," I said while meeting Chase's gaze out of the corner my eyes. "Those two were made for each other."

My friends continued to place bets about how long the marriage would last, and I gracefully bowed out of that conversation. I was more concerned with what Chase and Ginger were discussing. She had gone from sulking to happy pretty quickly, and all because her big brother was finally paying her some attention.

Every once in a while, however, Ginger glared at me. It was apparent that I'd be hearing about this, later on, be it at work or over the phone. She was a good person with a big heart, just a bit of a drama queen. Her clients at the spa loved her over-the-top personality. But I knew that the second we were alone, she would rip me a new asshole while complaining that I had "stolen" her date for most of the reception.

Maybe I was a bit too judgmental, though. Perhaps I shouldn't have spent so much time dancing with Chase since he did come with Ginger, but he was her brother for crying out loud! She acted as the two of them were on an actual date, which caused me to shiver in my seat. One of my friends at the table asked if I was feeling all right.

"Oh, yeah. I'm fine. The chicken just isn't sitting too well with me."

They all nodded in agreement, complaining that it was too salty and shouldn't have had so much cheese. Actually, the chicken was delicious, and I would have loved to have gotten seconds.

I'm shivering because Ginger is a little too obsessed with her big brother.

Each time a song ended, Chase tried to pull away from Ginger and make his way over to me. But she kept her hand on his and yanked it back, making it clear that he was *only* going to spend time with her the rest of the night. And every time he gave me an "I'm sorry" look, I forced myself to smile.

But inside, I was just as miserable as Ginger had been while watching us dance.

By the time the reception was winding down, I had watched the two of them dance to nearly a dozen songs while I had an extra few slices of wedding cake and too much champagne. They made their way over to me, but Ginger stood between us once again.

"Are you ready to head out, Margo? Because Chase and I are exhausted from all of the dancing. Did you see us on the floor? Isn't my big brother just the *best* dancer?" She was laying it on thick for some reason.

I started to feel sick to my stomach again but found a way to be fake. "I sure did, Ginger. You two seemed to be having a lot of fun, and yes, Chase is one hell of a dancer."

We piled into the limo, and once again, Chase tried to sit next to me, and Ginger intervened. I was on the end with her in the middle with Chase on her other side.

And quite frankly, I was done being polite.

I stood up and shifted to the other side of the limo, where I sat down directly in front of them.

Ginger looked pissed. "What's wrong? Do I smell or something?"

"Of course you don't," I replied while meeting Chase's knowing glance. "I just want to give you two plenty of room. Don't want to be a third wheel on your date with your *brother*."

6

Chase

"What's your problem tonight, Margo? Chase was my date, remember?"

I smacked my face with the palm of my hand while Margo sat across from us with her legs crossed, angrily twirling her foot around. I knew this would happen. I knew the second we got into the limo that the two of them would start to bicker. Although, none of this was Margo's fault. Ginger was the one who had demanded that I dote on her all evening. Besides, how could Ginger *not* expect me to be attracted to Margo? If anything, it was her fault for having Margo ride along with us in the first place.

"Nothing's my problem, Ginger. You've just made it abundantly clear that you don't want anyone chatting with your brother but yourself."

"You make it sound so gross, as though a big brother saving his little sister from—"

"Saving you from what, Ginger? Being without a man at a wedding?" I gasped and covered my mouth with my hand and then rolled my eyes. "Oh, the horror!"

Ginger glared at Margo with such intensity that for a moment, I could tell that Margo was considering walking the rest of the way home. But she was wearing heels. I rolled down the window a little bit, making it clear that I didn't want any part of this argument while also getting some much-needed fresh air. It was beautiful in Miami Beach, with the nearly full moon casting light down onto the ocean. People were walking along the sidewalks in South Beach, enjoying the night air while I was stuck listening to my younger sister act like a brat.

I would have loved to have been outside walking along Ocean Drive myself, but only if Margo joined me.

"Look, I'm sorry, Margo. I'm sure it wasn't easy going to this wedding all by yourself. Wait, I have an idea! You should talk to Chase's friend Jorge. He's just your type!"

Margo and I both glared at Ginger, leaving me no choice but to interject into an otherwise awkward conversation. I couldn't see Margo going for a guy like Jorge, nor did I want to see him attempt to make it happen.

"No, I don't think Jorge is Margo's type."

Ginger waved her hand at me in disgust. "How would you

know what Margo's type is when you just met her? Besides, he's your best friend. Sounds as though you don't think very highly of your own best friend, Chase."

"Why don't you worry about your friends, Ginger, and I'll worry about mine."

My God, I feel like I'm back in high school! When will she ever grow up?

Margo leaned forward toward Ginger. "Didn't you say that Jorge was boring?"

"Well, maybe I shouldn't have used that word. Jorge is just more low-key like you are."

That was all Margo needed to hear to end the conversation. Ginger folded her arms across her chest again, signaling to all of us that she was in a bad mood and had enough. Whereas Margo stared out my open window, eager for the driver to take her home.

I hated having to belittle my sister, but she had pushed me too damn far.

"You're acting like a spoiled brat, Ginger. It's time for you to act your age for a change. I can't say that I regret going to this wedding, but I do regret coming as your date."

And just as Ginger's mouth fell open, the driver pulled up to Margo's apartment complex. Margo dug into her clutch for her keys as the driver opened the door. "Well, this has been fairly awkward. Enjoy the rest of your evening, and it was a pleasure to meet you, Chase."

Ginger and I refused to speak to each other for several minutes until the driver pulled up to a stoplight not to far from Ginger's place. "So, are you interested in Margo or something?"

I shifted in my seat a little bit, wondering how to broach the subject of potentially dating my younger sister's best friend. "Yeah, I am. Margo is a classy lady, Ginger, and seems to have her life together. You don't meet women like her that often."

Ginger squinted her eyes at me, and after refusing to speak, I let out a sigh.

"And yes, I'm also physically attracted to her. Look, you're my sister, so this is weird to talk about with you."

"Well, you're not wrong. Margo is gorgeous. Honestly, I'm a bit jealous of her looks."

I squeezed her palm before kissing her on the cheek. "You have nothing to be jealous about. Good looks run in our family. Just out of curiosity, why didn't you introduce us before?"

Ginger searched my face a few moments before answering my question. "Because she's not the girl for you, and that's all you need to know." She yanked her hand away and turned back around, her eyes focused on the road ahead.

"What do you mean she's not the girl for me?"

"Just leave Margo alone, that's all I'm asking you to do. Besides, you're too old for her, and she's a bit naïve at times. So please don't think that she has her life together."

I turned my entire body toward my sister, demanding that she tell me the truth. "That's not why you didn't introduce us sooner, Ginger. And I know she's not that naïve because I spoke with her all evening."

She shot me a nasty look. "Yes, I know you spoke with her all evening! Look, you want the truth? Margo's a good girl. Yes, I owe her an apology for my behavior, but she's still my best friend."

I jokingly put my hand to my heart, pretending as though she had stabbed me. "That comment hurt, Ginger. Are you suggesting that I don't have what it takes to be a good boyfriend? Because if you are, that's messed up. Just because I've made some mistakes in the past doesn't mean that I haven't changed."

Ginger swatted at me, causing me to duck and miss. "Just stay away from Margo. Do I make myself clear?"

I shook my head in defiance. "Nope. Perhaps you've forgotten that I'm a grown-ass man who can make my own decisions in life, and that includes which women I choose to pursue. So you can sit there and pout all you like, but if I want to date Margo, then I'm going to date Margo, and there's nothing you can do about it.'

Ginger put her hands on her hips and glared at me, once again. "As your little sister, I forbid you to go after Margo! I saw the way you looked at her the second you laid eyes on her. The two of you acted as though you were the only ones in the room, and I know what'll happen if you get too close to her."

I wasn't expecting Ginger to be so protective of her friend, especially after being jealous of her all evening. Now I wondered if it wasn't jealousy but my sister's attempt at shielding Margo...from me. "You need to calm down. Besides, you're reading too much into the situation. I was just friendly with Margo because she didn't have a date. I mean, you yourself didn't want to show up without a date so badly that you asked me."

Ginger leaned back and let out a sigh. "Whatever, loser. Just stay far away from Margo and you'll never have to hear me complain about it again. And I know what I saw on the dance floor, Chase. I've also witnessed what your version of friendly evolves into. Believe me when I say that she's not the one for you."

I pondered what she could mean by that, "not the one for you," but nothing came to mind. All I could assume was that she didn't want me to hurt Margo. At any rate, my sister had stopped barking, so I decided not to pursue the matter.

"So, did you have a good time tonight?"

Ginger's body seemed to relax a little bit. "It was all right. I would have had a better time if you had danced with me more, though."

"We danced for almost twelve songs, Ginger! What more do you want from me?"

She shrugged while pulling out her phone to check her social media.

I will never understand women.

The limo pulled up to Ginger's place, where she gave me a quick peck on the cheek before getting out. My driver met my gaze in the rearview mirror, and since the partition had been down the whole evening, he must have heard our entire conversation.

"Take me home, man. Far, far away from my sister."

He chuckled as we made our way back into traffic, where I leaned against the back of the seat and closed my eyes. The whole evening had been a whirlwind of events. From the moment I had seen Margo, I had wanted to get to know her. There was a magnetic attraction between us that I knew she also felt. Her body pushed up against mine while we were dancing, her gorgeous smile, and that soft skin had my mind all jumbled.

I had been around plenty of gorgeous women before, especially since I traveled so much, but nobody had ever had that effect on me. I needed to know what drew me to her. I was going to find out despite my sister's request. Even as I was dancing with Ginger, there was a pull between Margo and me. I saw the sadness in her eyes as she watched us on the dance floor, and at that moment, I had never hated my sister so much.

Before that night, I had been depressed for quite some time. Lonely. People assumed that I must have been happy since I was successful. But I had been in a dark place ever since Amber had broken up with me; drinking too much and falling asleep on the couch. In business meetings and with friends and family, I was all smiles. But behind closed doors, I was an emotional mess.

All of that seemed to fade tonight as I was dancing with Margo. I completely forgot that I would be going back to an empty house and that my ex-girlfriend was on her honeymoon. All that mattered was that Margo had been in my arms, and I desperately needed to experience it again.

Ginger had made it abundantly clear, however, that it would not be happening. I understood my sister's apprehension on some level, but she had to let Margo make her own decisions.

I opened my eyes while reaching for a bottle of water, and that's when I saw it: Margo's clutch, laying on the seat across from me. She must have been so eager to get away from Ginger that she had completely forgotten about it after she pulled out her keys.

I reached for her clutch and promptly opened it up. It wasn't large, so I assumed nothing too important would be inside. All I found was a wad of cash, a tube of mascara, some blush, lipstick, and those rice paper sheets that she had used to blot the oil from her face.

In other words, nothing significant that she'd need right away.

I held the clutch as my driver headed toward my mansion.

This is fantastic. Now I have an excuse to see Margo without Ginger around and for a good reason. Surely my sister won't be upset at my returning her best friend's purse. Not to mention that when I show up at her place, Margo will be alone.

Bingo.

7

Margo

My back hit the front door as soon as it slammed shut, and I didn't move until the sound of the limo driving away filled my otherwise quiet apartment. After letting out a long sigh, I slid my aching feet out of my high heels and stumbled into the kitchen, where my face hit the palm of my hands at the table.

I was a complete mess inside.

Ginger's big brother was precisely the kind of guy I was attracted to. He was tall, dark, and handsome. Or as Guadalupe would say, *alto, oscuro y guapo*.

There was no denying the mutual attraction between us, either. Chase hadn't kept his eyes off of me for most of the night, including the wedding ceremony. He probably didn't think I had noticed, but he focused on me the entire time. And after having my heart ripped apart by Nick, I embraced the ego boost.

As the pain in my feet started to subside, I ransacked the refrigerator for a late-night snack. Anything to squash the butterflies that were fluttering a mile a minute within my stomach. It felt as though I were walking on air. I planned on forgetting all about Chase after the wedding and reception and just chalking it up to a fun experience. But then he had to impress me with his dancing skills, and about halfway through the first song, I was emotionally invested in the man.

The turkey, provolone, and pesto sandwich I made wasn't half-bad, but it didn't take care of the butterflies in my stomach.

Ginger had mentioned her brother on a few occasions, but we'd only been friends for about a year, and therefore, I'd never thought about meeting him. Not to mention, that at the time, I was involved with Nick, who, at that very moment, was probably with one of his many girlfriends.

I washed the rest of my sandwich down with some water and then headed into the bathroom to remove all of my makeup.

Chase was either one of those charming men who could make any woman feel special, or we just had great chemistry. Regardless of the reason, I went from wanting nothing to do with men for a while to not being able to think about anything other than Ginger's older brother.

And knowing that she wasn't keen on us even chatting with each other made it even worse.

I stripped down to just my panties, put on a tiny tank top, and then climbed into bed, hoping that a good night's rest would cure my obsession. But it was a good hour before I could even fall asleep, despite being exhausted. If I hadn't been with Chase all evening, then it wouldn't have taken me more than a few minutes to nod off after the long day I'd had.

The only thing that I dreamed about that night was Chase with his hands wrapped around my waist as we waltzed effortlessly across the dance floor.

I WOKE UP TO THE BIRDS CHIRPING RIGHT OUTSIDE OF MY window on the balcony attached to my bedroom. I also woke up with a smile on my face and more butterflies in my stomach, thanks to dreaming about Chase all night.

It had been a long time since I dreamed about a man in a positive way. After Nick had broken up with me, I had recurring nightmares that involved me walking in on him cheating on me. But last night, it was all about Chase and me dancing, followed by dinner at an expensive restaurant, and then going for a walk along the beach. The two of us sat down on the sand and watched the waves crash in, our feet getting wet as we looked up at the full moon.

But I had just gotten out of a relationship, so naturally, I was a bit apprehensive. I also wasn't sure how strongly Chase felt about me. Maybe it was nothing but a fun night of dancing to him, or maybe he was sitting at home feeling the same way about me. Whatever his feelings were, I was now over Nick and growing more obsessed with Chase by the minute. I wanted to feel my body pressed against his again, to smell his intoxicating aroma, and just see if we had enough chemistry to pursue a relationship.

Physically I was drained, but emotionally I was on cloud nine. Being at a wedding was a bit more work than I had anticipated, and I could have used an extra day off to recuperate. I silently chastised myself for not requesting today off and made a mental note to do so if I was ever asked to be a bridesmaid again. The photo sessions, visiting with guests, and working to ensure the ceremony was as picture perfect as it could be was definitely exhausting.

My hand groggily reached for my cellphone on the nightstand, checking to see if anyone had texted me. I half-expected Ginger to send me an "I'm sorry" message about her obnoxious, childlike behavior at the wedding, but of course, she hadn't. She was probably waiting to corner me at the spa, where she'd give me every reason in the world not to date her older brother.

The only message I had was from work. My first client had canceled her appointment, and I wasn't needed until noon.

"Well, thank goodness," I said to myself while sliding out of bed.

A booked schedule meant more money in my pocket, but

my body appreciated being able to relax a little longer this morning. I popped a few aspirin while brewing some coffee, then opened my kitchen blinds. The bright Miami sunshine poured into my apartment. Usually, I'd embrace it, but it was a bit much for someone dealing with a slight hangover.

The butterflies resumed their fluttering as I waited for my coffee to brew. All I could think about was Chase and wondered if and when I'd see him again. If Ginger hadn't done everything in her power to keep us apart, then maybe he'd have asked me for my number or even a date.

Just as I sat down with my morning cup of coffee, someone knocked on my door. The only people who ever came to visit unannounced were my best friends and family, so I didn't bother putting on a robe.

I took a big sip of my coffee and then opened the door, not even asking who it was or looking through the peephole. Chase's eyes met mine as soon as it opened, and I almost dropped my full coffee cup onto the floor.

"Oh, Chase! Hi!"

When he looked me up and down, I suddenly remembered that I was only wearing a pair of pink lace booty shorts and a white tank top. As my free hand clutched my chest, Chase started to laugh, and I struggled to think of my next move.

Of course, I answer the door without a bra or pants on!

I reached into my hallway closet and grabbed the first jacket, hanging it haphazardly across my chest. Chase continued to laugh as my knees buckled together, and it wasn't until he handed me my clutch that I started to calm down a little bit.

"You left this in the limo last night."

Sparks went through my body as my hands caressed his, taking the clutch while simultaneously holding onto my coffee and covering up my body. "Thank you. Wow, I didn't even realize I had left it behind."

Chase cocked his head at me and revealed his gorgeous smile once again. "You just now realized that you didn't have your clutch? How much champagne did you drink last night?"

I tilted my head and shrugged, still embarrassed that he had seen me half-naked, especially after the intense dreams I'd had about him last night, which featured us tangled up in each other's arms. The longer he stared at me, the more convinced I was that he could read my mind and knew that I had dirty fantasies about him.

He cleared his throat and glanced at my coffee mug. "That coffee sure does smell good."

"Oh, thanks! It's an espresso blend from this local coffee beanery. Although, it's nothing compared to what Guadalupe makes for us down at the spa."

Chase dug his hands into his pockets while casually leaning against the door, and that's when it hit me.

"Would you like to come in for a cup of coffee? I made a whole pot."

"I thought you'd never ask."

Once Chase was inside, I excused myself and rushed into

my bedroom, where I promptly slid into a pair of jean shorts, a bra, and a pink tank top.

"Sorry for looking like a hot mess when I answered the door," I said while walking into the kitchen. "Cream and sugar?"

"No apologies necessary. I take it black, thanks."

We sat down on my couch while nervously sipping coffee, and once again, there was that magnetic attraction.

I couldn't take the silence anymore. "Last night was so much fun. Thanks again for dancing with me."

"It was my pleasure. So, this is quite the place you have here."

I leaned back against the couch a little bit, doing my best to seem relaxed despite being a ball of nerves. "Thank you. I moved here about a year ago, right after Lavender Dreams Spa hired me. I absolutely love it."

Chase turned to look out the window directly behind us, which faced the ocean. "There's nothing quite like waking up to that view, is there? My place has a similar view, and I wouldn't have it any other way. Hurricanes aside, of course."

I laughed as he leaned back against the couch, both of us resting our head in our hands while staring at each other. Chase had the most gorgeous set of lips. "Eh, every climate has its fair share of extreme weather. What did you think of the band last night?"

"They were pretty good. It's been a long time since I danced."

"Well," I said while leaning in a little bit, "you wouldn't have known by the way you moved last night."

Chase playfully brushed a lock of hair from out of my face. "You're too kind, Margo. So, are you working today?"

I took a big sip of my coffee, suddenly aware that my hangover required more caffeine. "Yep. My first client canceled, which sucks, but I also appreciate the extra time it gives me. I have a noon color and a cut. What are your plans for today?"

"I have a few business calls to make, but then I'll probably spend the afternoon relaxing. Not sure if I told you, but I travel a lot on my job, and it can get pretty tiring. Don't get me wrong, I enjoy seeing different parts of the country, but I need a day just to relax."

"I completely know what you mean. Well, except for traveling the world part. My job keeps me right here unless some famous person suddenly wants me to do their hair and makeup."

Chase placed his empty coffee mug onto the table and then looked me dead in the eyes. "I'm just going to come right out with it, Margo. I had the time of my life last night, and I really want to see you again."

I could feel myself turning the deepest shade of red possible. "I'd like that too, Chase. Last night was a lot of fun, wasn't it? I mean, meeting you was a lot of fun."

"Truth be told, it's been a long time since I've connected with someone so quickly. Would you like to have dinner with me next Friday night?"

Without even checking to see if I had any evening appointments at the salon, I nodded. “I’d love to.”

“Perfect. I think we’ll have an even better time...being alone together.”

I walked him to the door, and once again, after it shut, my back hit it. But this time, I slid all the way down until I was sitting on the floor.

It was going to be impossible to think about anything else besides Chase all week.

8

Chase

Jorge and I were hanging out in his penthouse apartment, which he often referred to as his "man cave in the sky," although I had told him that was redundant. His whole place was a man cave with droves of women coming and going all of the time. It was pretty nice, though. On one end was a pool table and mini-bar, and the end we were on had a modern-sectional and eighty-inch ultra-high-definition television mounted on the wall.

Jorge kept changing the channels until he finally landed on baseball, then looked at me for approval. I just shrugged at him, though, since I wasn't in the mood to watch TV.

"Dude, even I don't have an eighty-inch television in my house and I design the things."

We got together every Wednesday night to have a few drinks, catch up on each other's lives, and shoot the shit. We discussed our careers, and I was eager to tell him about how things were going with my company lately.

"Everything is looking up, Jorge. And by everything, I mean all of my products. Laptops, televisions, home security systems—nothing but profits, profits, profits. I won't have to worry about cash flow for a long time."

Jorge held his beer out to me as a way of saluting. "Good for you, man. You certainly bust your ass off trying to get ahead, and I have yet to see you fail. Have you been in touch with anyone from college lately?"

We had met at the University of Miami, where we shared an obsession for the Miami Hurricanes football team. "No, aside from seeing the typical engagement announcements on my social media timelines. Everybody's been tying the knot lately. It's crazy."

"Well, that's what happens when you get to be our age. Just take a look at Paris and John. That was one hell of a wedding, huh?"

My body tensed a bit, remembering how Jorge's hands had started to go down to my sister's ass. "It certainly was a good time."

"I have to admit," Jorge said while leaning forward on his knees, "I was a bit disappointed that I couldn't have spent more time with Ginger."

"I bet you were," I said while giving him a knowing glance.

But he held up his hands, signaling that it wasn't what I

was thinking. "You made your point clear, man. But she seemed a bit preoccupied with the way you were chatting up Margo. If I didn't know any better, I'd say that she was jealous of the two of you."

I chugged the rest of my beer, remembering how bratty Ginger had acted at the reception. I was beyond embarrassed. "What can I say? My sister is overbearing."

Jorge wasn't taking that for a final answer, though. "So, what's the deal between you and Margo?"

"She's a beautiful woman, Jorge. Who wouldn't be attracted to her?"

"I knew it, man," he said while also chugging the rest of his beer. "So, is Margo going to be Amber 2.0? Do I see a relationship on the horizon?"

It wasn't Jorge's fault for offending me with that comment. I had kept my depression over Amber a secret, not wanting anyone to see someone as masculine as myself getting upset over a woman.

"Actually, I'm not in that kind of mindset right now, man. Just because I was with Amber for so long doesn't mean I want to dive right into another relationship."

Jorge just shook his head at me, refusing to believe it. "Bullshit. I know you too well, Chase. It's how you're wired."

I reached into the nearby mini-fridge, popped the top off of another beer, and nodded while taking a long sip. "All right, fine. I asked Margo out to dinner. But that's it, just dinner. I'm not going to rush into anything. Besides, my schedule is jam-packed as it is. I barely have time to use the bathroom between business meetings."

Jorge slapped me hard on the shoulder, causing me to wince in pain. "I can't believe you're going for it with your sister's best friend! Talk about having guts. I'm surprised Ginger's even letting you go through with this. You know, since she's so ahhh...overbearing."

"There's just something about Margo that I can't shake, Jorge. I know I'd regret it if I didn't at least ask her out."

"Once you shag her, bro, there won't be anything left to shake!"

The verbiage Jorge used could be downright disgusting at times. "'Shag,' Jorge? Really?"

He just rolled his eyes at me. "Need I remind you about some of the girls you hooked up with back in college? But, hey, nothing but respect on my part man. Good for you. That's what men are supposed to do, right?"

"We haven't been in college for a long time, Jorge. Those days are long behind me."

"You know what I'm talking about, Chase. Once you have sex with a woman, the spark is gone. It's just a cold, hard fact. Women act like we're supposed to marry them just because we've had sex, but that's bullshit. I want a passionate life, and eventually, it dies out in a relationship."

As I nursed my beer, I couldn't help but wonder if there were any validity to what Jorge said. Was this just a raw, animal, sexual attraction that, once fulfilled, would disappear into thin air? Or could something more serious develop between Margo and me?

"I'm not like that anymore, Jorge. Not that I'm going balls-deep into a relationship with Margo, but I'm much different than I was back in college."

"Whatever, man. You know what I'm saying. But isn't Margo a lot younger than you, too?"

"Yeah, she's about eight years younger than me. So what? We're both adults."

Jorge nodded while staring at the television, which he kept muted the entire evening. "That's true, and Margo does seem like a nice chick. Hey, you've got nothing to lose over dinner, right?"

My intuition had made me billions of dollars over the years. I knew when to walk away from a business deal and when to go for one. Needless to say, I was an excellent judge of character. But when it came to women, maybe I needed to be more like Jorge. Perhaps he saw something in her that I didn't, something that suggested we wouldn't be more than a fling.

As I began thinking about what Jorge had suggested, that Margo and I would just fool around, I also thought about what Ginger had said in the limo after the reception. After throwing a hissy fit, she point-blank said that Margo wasn't the right girl for me.

Whatever.

As I finished the rest of my beer, Jorge ran his hands through his hair, and I instantly knew what he was about to ask me. He had the same look on his face whenever he approached a girl at a bar.

"So, I'm just gonna come right out and ask you. Can I get Ginger's number?"

The look I gave him should have sent him running, but Jorge was on a mission. "Absolutely not. Look, she literally just got dumped by some guy she thought was *the one*, and I'm gonna be straight-up with you, Jorge. You're a billionaire playboy. You're the complete opposite of what my sister both wants and deserves."

Jorge threw both of his hands at me, as though he were chucking a basketball. "Whatever, man. If I'm such a jerk, then why are we best friends?"

"You're not a jerk," I said with slight remorse, "but you're still in that stage where you don't want to settle down. If you want to go out and hook up with women who know you'll never call them again, that's perfectly fine. But I know for a fact that my sister is *not* that kind of a woman. Besides, she's too busy studying for her MBA finals right now."

"You're assuming that I only want to fool around with Ginger. What if I want to date her?"

"Dude, you just told me that you wanted a passionate life and that passion dies, which is why you dump women. Why the hell would I give you my little sister's phone number?"

Jorge's ego had been sufficiently bruised. "You should just hang a sign around my neck that says 'undateable.'"

"I'll tell you what," I said with a chuckle, "I'll give Ginger *your* number. Let her be the one who decides what she wants. Deal?"

"Are you going to tell her what I'm like ahead of time, though? Because if you are, that's not fair."

"Are *you* going to tell her that you don't stay in relationships after the passion has died? Because if you aren't, that's not fair either. So, do we have a deal?"

Jorge shrugged and let out an obnoxious sigh. "Deal."

We spent the rest of the evening just shooting the shit, talking about work, our college days, and commenting about the wedding. But my mind kept going back to Margo. She looked so sexy first thing in the morning that I wanted to see her that way every morning. The way she reached for a jacket was so awkward and adorable. With someone like Margo, I could see the passion between us lasting for an incredibly long time. She seemed to have one of those personalities that kept you guessing what she'd do or say next.

Only time would tell, though, and there was no point in worrying.

Even if it ended up being a fling, then it would probably end up being the best one of my life.

9

Margo

It was getting close to seven o'clock on Friday night, and my stomach had turned into a swarm of butterflies once again. I had changed my outfit five times before finally deciding on a white silk dress, one that would be suitable for both a low-key and upscale restaurant. Chase didn't tell me where we were going, which only put more stress on me to look my best. If he took me to an outdoor cafe where we could dance under the moonlight, hopefully near the beach, my beige sandals would be comfortable enough.

And if he took me to an intimate restaurant, the same sandals would slide up and down his legs underneath the table.

What has gotten into you, Margo?

It wasn't like me to be so flirtatious. Up until I moved to Florida to attend cosmetology school, I had led a pretty sheltered life. I just wasn't wired to go out clubbing, trying to hook up with a different guy every night while fighting to remember their names the next day.

And as I struggled to choose a matching handbag, I remembered that it brought up another issue—my virginity.

My parents raised me to wait for the right guy, and even when I was attending college and dating guys, I had never found one who seemed worthy of taking it from me. It's not that I never had any sexual desires, either; in fact, it was quite the opposite. Not finding a man worthy of my time was beginning to get on my nerves, and the longer I waited, the more I wanted it to happen.

But only with a man who didn't view me as a mattress to sleep against at night.

I decided to go with a pink handbag embellished with a few white flowers. The white flowers would go well with my dress, while the pink brought out my blush and lipstick.

I also dabbed some coconut-scented body spray on my neck and wrists, which seemed perfect for a night on the town in Key Biscayne.

And then I sat down on the couch and waited for Chase to show, unable to turn off the wheel of thoughts running through my mind. My intuition kept telling me to take things slow with him, but something told me that guys like him didn't move slow. They went for what they wanted in life, and fast. I had been down this road before with other guys, and it always ended badly.

Before Nick there was Keith, and before Keith there was Pat, and before Pat there was Garrett. Every single one of them had crushed my heart, and with the exception of Nick, it had taken me months to get over them. I could see that happening with Chase. Not because he gave me any reason to doubt his intentions, but because the magnetic pull between us was so strong. I had felt it between my legs that night on the dance floor.

Will I give my virginity to Chase? What if he stands me up tonight? Is he going to break my heart?

There was something dangerous about Chase that stood out to me, but I couldn't quite put my finger on it. He had been nothing short of a gentleman at the reception, but the look in his eyes screamed "heartbreaker." I could see myself falling head over heels in love with him...and then sobbing into my pillow after he broke my heart.

I shook my head and silently told myself to get a grip. My mother was always telling me not to project, and just to let life play itself out. A seemingly nice guy was about to take me out to dinner, so I should just take it for what it was and enjoy the evening. He was incredibly good looking, had eyes that pierced my soul, and a chiseled jawbone that made my knees weak. But that didn't necessarily mean he was a heartbreaker. Maybe Chase would end up being a great guy who didn't treat me the way Nick and all of the others had.

Or maybe he'd be worse. Perhaps he'd wine and dine me,

take what he wanted, and then leave me crying and begging for more while laughing. Guys could be quite cruel.

My head jolted up as soon as the doorbell rang, and I nearly tripped on the rug as I went to answer it. I opened the door to see Chase standing on the other side of it, wearing an all-black ensemble, including his shoes. My mouth fell open as he smiled at me, revealing bright-white teeth that were a stark but sexy contrast against his black suit, shirt, pants, and tie. The entire look also made his eyes pop, and as a result, I had to steady myself against the door.

"Um, hi," I whispered.

Chase looked equally impressed with my outfit. "That's, um, quite the dress you have on this evening."

I reached down and straightened it out a bit. "Oh, thank you. I wasn't sure where you'd be taking me, but I figured this would work well in any type of setting. Unless you don't think it will, in which case I can—"

Chase laughed while holding up his hand. "You look perfect for where we're going tonight, Margo. In fact, you'd look perfect in just about anything."

The two of us smiled at each other for several long seconds, until he finally reached out his hand, and I took it.

He held the door open to his black Rolls Royce, and my body sank into the soft, comfortable black leather seat.

"With all due respect, this is one hell of a car."

He gave me a smile that instantly melted my heart, shifted the car into gear, and then seamlessly began driving. "Thank you. Do you enjoy seafood, Margo?"

My stomach growled while picturing being served a massive lobster, and then drenching it in butter. "No, I *love* seafood!"

"Great, because I reserved a table for us at Seafood Nouveau in Key Biscayne."

I can't even afford a salad at that place.

Seafood Nouveau was an open-concept restaurant that looked directly out onto the ocean. They prided themselves on only serving seafood caught fresh that day, straight out of the Atlantic ocean. The hostess sat us outside on the patio, and a waiter immediately brought over an expensive bottle of champagne.

"The usual, Mr. Bowers?"

Chase nodded at the server, and he proceeded to pour each of us a glass of champagne. Chase's eyes seemed to light up the longer he stared into mine, and as he raised his glass to mine, I felt as though I could melt right into his arms.

"This is my favorite champagne, and I had a bottle reserved for us ahead of time."

I drank the sweet elixir and nearly downed it in one gulp, only stopping when I realized that it wouldn't have been very ladylike. "I can see why, Chase. This is delicious."

We silently looked over the menu. I wanted to gasp at how expensive everything was but kept that to myself. I was sure Chase knew I didn't make nearly as much money as he did.

Chase and I spent the rest of the evening getting to know each other, and I couldn't remember the last time that I had connected so well with somebody. He was surprised by my love of football too.

"I'm a huge football fan, although I didn't get into it until I was in college."

He washed his lobster down with more champagne as his foot played with mine. "Who's your favorite team?"

"The Miami Hurricanes, of course."

That seemed to impress him quite a bit. "Well, then I'll have to take you to a game sometime because that just so happens to be my favorite team too."

The women around us, even those who were with their husbands, kept looking over at Chase. I couldn't blame them one bit. He was the kind of man who demanded attention from the entire room, especially since he was wearing all black. I suspected the outfit was from a high-end designer.

"If you don't mind me asking, is that a Gucci suit?"

Chase proudly opened up his blazer to display the logo, and I couldn't help but lean across the table to get a better look. "You have a good eye for fashion, I see. Although the tie isn't Gucci."

Feeling brave from all of the flirting and champagne, I lifted it to get a look at the label. "Armani Exchange. Very nice."

Our eyes locked with intensity as I continued to lean across the table, only retreating to my seat when the waiter came over.

"How is everything here?"

Chase answered the waiter without taking his eyes off of me. "Everything's perfect, thank you."

Both of our feet were flirting with each other underneath the table at that point, and I found myself entirely hypnotized by Chase Bowers. Not only was he physically one of the most gorgeous men I had ever seen, but his attitude was both magnetic and dangerous. He wasn't a man who took "no" for an answer, and yet he spoke with me in a soft, velvety-like tone.

"This lobster is delicious, by the way."

"They catch it fresh from the ocean daily. If you get up early enough, you can actually see their lobster boats from my balcony."

"Are you an early bird?"

Chase shrugged while relaxing in his seat, giving me a better view of his gorgeous body. His Gucci suit clung nicely to his chest, highlighting his muscular abs that gave way to large muscles.

I want to dig my nails into his chest.

"It depends on what I had going on the day before, but I do enjoy seeing the sunrise. I especially like the morning fog that envelops Key Biscayne."

I couldn't take my eyes off of him. He spoke about the island with such love and admiration, and I pictured the two of us watching the sunrise together from his balcony. His foot found his way a little bit up my calf, causing me to giggle as people passed us.

"That sounds delightful."

"Speaking of delightful," Chase said while leaning across the table, "how about we go for a walk on the beach?"

My eyes searched his for a few moments, but it didn't take me long to agree.

After dinner, the two of us walked down to the beach, where we removed our shoes and skimmed our feet along the water. We didn't hold hands at first. We merely trekked barefoot along the sand, letting it mesh between our toes as we chatted about our own lives.

"I wish I had a sibling," I said as we approached a massive rock jutting out into the ocean.

"Well, it certainly makes things a bit less lonely when you have family around. But there's something to be said about sanity."

"Ginger does seem like a handful at times, and she's the same way at the spa."

Chase casually reached his hand out to mine, where our fingers seamlessly intertwined with each other.

"Do you enjoy what you do at the spa, Margo?" He stopped and turned to face me.

"I love my job and can't imagine doing anything else with my life."

Chase reached for my other hand. "If you had all of the money in the world, would you still be doing it, though?"

I pondered his question, wondering if there was a subtle meaning behind it. "Yes, I can honestly say that I would. I mean, obviously, I need money, but I get a lot of joy from being a beautician. Seeing my client's eyes light up after I've given them a new makeup look, a different hairstyle, or even just a cut that adds years to their life is so fulfilling to me. It's my calling in life."

He ran his hand through my hair as the waves crashed against the rock.

"That's real happiness, Margo. When you can look at your career and just know that you'd do it for free, that's the good stuff. Money is just a bonus."

As Chase continued to stare into my eyes, I accepted that if something serious morphs from this, all I could do was ride the waves.

10

Chase

The waves crashing against the jutting rock only heightened the sexual tension between Margo and me. Every collision caused my desire to swell, and as the cool evening breeze swept in, her coconut perfume wafted into my nose and awakened my senses. It might have been our very first date, but every part of me wanted to be inside of Margo.

Immediately.

We had walked far enough on the beach to be away from the watchful gaze of any onlookers, and truth be told, I'd never had sex outside before. Nor did I picture Margo being the kind of woman who had, either. But the longer we stared into each other's eyes, the more we needed to be physically connected.

I leaned forward, my feet sinking farther into the sand, and ran my hand alongside her face. She gazed back into my eyes, silently permitting me to move forward. As I bent to kiss her, a wave crashed so hard against the rock that some of the water splashed onto us, causing her white dress to become transparent. Our tongues intertwined with each other as my hands slowly slid the strap of her dress off, revealing her gorgeous, supple breasts.

Margo stood with her hands at her side, as I trailed my fingers down her arms. When I reached her wrists, I lifted them and encouraged her to wrap her arms around my neck. I dipped to meet her lips with mine, and slowly lowered us to the sand without breaking contact. She eased back, taking me with her. And once she got comfortable, I settled in on my side, still able to tease her lips and now able to explore her body. Her nipples hardened as I traced circles around them, and her skin pebbled when I drew abstract designs over her chest.

She pulled back long enough to find the top to my pants and then began kissing me again, while slowly unzipping them. My erection peered out through my boxers, and she gasped at the size. Within minutes her dress was gone, exposing all of her perfect body, revealing every soft, delicate curve that was the ideal contrast to my muscular physique. I tossed my jacket off to the side along with my shirt and her dress, and next went my pants.

I took the opportunity to reposition myself between her legs and settle on my elbow above her as the waves continued to hit the rock and sand. The night was perfect, the moon was bright, and the ocean provided a perfect symphony.

She was as intoxicated by the setting as I was by her, and the natural progression had led us to becoming one with the waves lapping at our feet and nature covering us with a blanket of darkness.

The heat between her legs welcomed me like we were old lovers, and I slid between her folds, moistening my shaft. Everything about her felt perfect against me from the warmth of her skin to the taste of her lips. As my tongue danced with hers, Margo dug her long, pink nails into my shoulder, driving me mad with need.

I couldn't hold back anymore.

Just as I positioned the head of my shaft against her core, Margo stopped and pulled back. Her hands landed firmly on my shoulders were she held me inches from her face.

"I'm a virgin." She blurted it out so fast that I couldn't believe what she'd said.

I instantly pulled back and rested on my knees in the sand, making sure I had heard her right. "You're a...what?"

Her shoulders dropped back, and she sighed. "A virgin, Chase. I'm a virgin."

As aggressively as I wanted to take her at that moment, I couldn't help but soften up a little bit inside. I couldn't believe that a woman as sexy and sophisticated as Margo had never had sex before. All I could do was maintain eye contact while thinking about what to do or say next.

"Margo, I, I mean...I had no idea."

She dropped her hands and pushed herself up onto her elbows and kissed me on the lips. That simple gesture pulled me right back into the moment I'd thought we'd lost. With my prick nestled right up against her pink pearl, it was so warm and wet that all I wanted to do was plunge deep inside and make love to her with the waves as our backdrop.

But she was a virgin, and I knew how special that was to women. It was usually different for men. We wanted to have sex as soon as possible, and preferably with plenty of women. But ladies such as Margo waited for a special occasion with a special man, and as the moonlight hit her face, it dawned on me—I was that special man.

That was a huge responsibility.

Sure, I wasn't a playboy like Jorge, but a virgin? This changed everything.

Margo sensed the hesitation in my voice and demeanor. "Please don't let that turn you off, Chase. You have no idea how long I've waited for this moment." She searched my eyes, almost pleading with me not to change my mind without saying a word.

I pointed to my package, which was still standing at attention, and grinned at her. "Does it look like it turned me off?"

Margo giggled a little bit before pulling me into another kiss, and if she didn't stop, then I knew it would happen. I was too aroused to back out of it now, but I needed to make sure before proceeding. It would absolutely be painful, but if she wanted to stop, I would stand up, help her get dressed, take her home, and kiss her goodnight. But God, I really hoped that wasn't what she wanted.

I pulled back and stared into her eyes, needing to see her truth. "Are you sure this is what you want, Margo? Right here, right now, the two of us on this beach? You've waited an awfully long time for this moment, and I don't want to ruin it for you." I kissed the tip of her nose and waited for her answer.

Her chest started to heave, her erect nipples brushed against me as the waves continued to crash onto the shore. As one big wave cascaded over our feet, she wrapped her arms around me and then used her feet to pull me closer, thereby burying my cock deep inside of her flower.

Margo was no longer a virgin.

I gave her a minute to adjust and watched her face for any sign of discomfort or regret. When I found neither, the man inside of me came alive. I took it slow, but deep, undulating my hips in time with the sounds of the surf—in and out—my massive shaft bringing out the woman in her. Margo's moans against the crashing waves sent tingles down my spine as my toes curled into the sand. I had never felt so alive as in the moment, becoming one with Margo under the full moon.

Just knowing that she had saved herself for this moment, and chose me of all people, made me want to give her the experience of a lifetime. Regardless of what happened between us, I wanted her to remember tonight as one filled with unbridled passion, and be confident she had made the right choice in saving herself.

I was naturally dominant, and with it being Margo's first time, I was grateful that she let me take charge. I wanted her to enjoy every minute of this and not worry about what would please me. The truth was, she could have just laid there without moving a muscle, and I would have been a happy man. Her gorgeous breasts swayed as I pushed into her, and I longed for the day when I could watch them bounce as she rode me, grabbing them as she took my length, sucking on them while she fucked me—but that would have to wait for another night.

The entire experience was slow, unhurried. I peppered her shoulders with open-mouthed kisses, and she dug her nails into my back when I'd hit that spot no man had ever touched. She was so responsive. Her back arched, and she let out these sexy moans that rode out to sea with the receding tide.

Margo moved in a way that encouraged me into the angles that hit the spots that made her soar, and she encouraged me with her hands, and her feet, and her mouth all over my body. She was a woman who knew what she wanted despite not having any experience getting it. I fit perfectly inside of her, as though our parts were made for each other.

With one roll of my hips and a deep thrust, Margo tossed her head back and screamed so loudly that I was afraid we were going to get caught, but the passion between us was far too intense just to stop. Both of us needed to climax, to finish what we had started, before leaving the beach. I made love to her the best way that I knew how, kissing every inch of her body as she prepared to surrender herself to me. And as her core flooded with lubrication, I knew she was almost there. I wanted to make Margo come so hard that her eyes rolled into the back of her head, and she screamed my name so loud that it bounced off of the rocks.

My orgasm was starting to build, and I wouldn't last much longer.

I broke our kiss so I could meet her eyes. I wanted to watch as she came apart, to commit it to memory. With my hands cradling her jaw, and my stare locked on her, she squeezed me from the inside out. Her moans intensified as I pushed us to the brink of an orgasm, and even though I was ready to release, I waited for her.

Margo's lips parted, and I could tell that it was about to happen. As we stared into each other's eyes, both of us cried out with pleasure as the waves around us crested, so did our ecstasy. Her body convulsed right along with mine. I tipped my forehead to hers while I waited for us both to come down, and then I rolled onto my back and cradled Margo against my side with my arm.

Both of us were exhausted, and I could have easily fallen asleep, but I wanted to make sure she was all right. I needed to know she didn't regret what had just happened and that it was everything she had hoped it would be. And I realized that I hoped it meant as much to her as it had to me.

I looked down to see her smiling, the light of the moon bouncing off of her eyes.

"Thank you," she whispered.

I knew she would remember that night for the rest of her life.

As would I.

❧ 11 ❧

Margo

It was unbelievably hard to focus on anything at work. I kept replaying what had happened between Chase and me on the beach the other night. Before he had picked me up, I genuinely hadn't expected to give myself to him—well, not that night. Sure, it was in the back of my mind that something could happen, but never that quickly.

There was just no denying our sexual chemistry.

As one of my clients waited for her highlights to set, Ginger called me over to the desk.

"What's up?"

"You tell me, Margo. You're just gazing out into space between clients. Is anything wrong?"

I just shook my head while going back to check on my client's highlights, and then made my way over to where someone needed their eyebrows waxed. I stared into the hot wax for several minutes before finally remembering what it was that I needed to do. Even the client gave me a double-take, silently wondering if she had made the right decision when choosing a stylist.

Ginger kept checking clients in as I tried to stay on track, but I kept thinking about how I was no longer a virgin. Chase had taken it from me. Well, I didn't want to put it so bluntly. I had given him my virginity sounded much better, and I didn't have any regrets about it. From the moment we started walking along the beach, I somehow just knew he would be the one.

"Margo, I think her highlights are done."

I ran over to the client and checked, and sure enough, they were ready. "Thanks," I yelled over to Ginger.

I continued running around the salon that morning, forgetting how to perform basic tasks such as shampooing, trimming bangs, and applying makeup. It was as though all of my years of cosmetology school had gone down the drain, and to make matters worse, Ginger was a witness to it all.

Every once in a while, I'd look up at her, just to see her shaking her head before proceeding to either check someone in or cash someone out. I couldn't tell her about it either since it was her brother, and I knew she didn't want us dating. If she ever found out that I had gone on a date with him, let alone that he was the first guy I ever had sex with, I didn't even want to know what would happen.

"Margo? Margo? Margo!"

I looked up from the washing station to see Ginger flagging me down. One of the new hairstylists came over and offered to finish shampooing to see what Ginger needed.

"What's wrong, Ginger?"

"Your last client of the day just canceled because her cat needs to go to the vet. What's wrong with you, anyway? You keep dazing off."

"Nothing," I lied. "I'm just a bit tired."

"Well, just don't give someone a highlight who only wants a cut. That's one way to flush your career down the toilet."

I rolled my eyes while making my way back to my station. The new hairstylist did a great job of shampooing and conditioning the hair, although, given the coarse texture, I would have used something a bit more moisturizing. The woman smiled at me as our eyes met in the mirror.

"So, you want a new hair color today, right? Are you looking to go darker or lighter?"

She just about fell out of the chair. "Are you crazy, lady? I just need my hair trimmed. Don't even touch the color! I've been a brunette all of my life, and I'm not interested in any services you're trying to sell me!"

Her screams caught the attention of everyone in the salon, including Guadalupe, who was making her way over. That was the last thing I needed. I took tremendous pride in my work, and after one verbal mistake, one of the salon owners had overheard.

"Is everything all right, miss?"

The woman ripped the black smock off and stood up, towering over poor Guadalupe.

"This dingbat was going to color my hair when all I signed up for was a trim. Is this how you get people to spend more money? Because my sisters and I come here all of the time, so believe me, you get plenty of money from me!"

Guadalupe put her arm around the client and walked her outside the salon, but not before turning around to give me an "it's okay, dear" look.

I could deal with snotty clients, but I couldn't handle letting down Guadalupe. Ever since I had started there a few months ago, she was always singing my praises. She constantly told me I was one of the best that she had, and even though I wanted to be modest, I wanted to believe her. I knew what the hell I was doing when it came to my job. In fact, I had only had two complaints, and both were from women who complained about everyone.

I walked over to Ginger and sat down in the seat next to her. "All right, I was lying to you before. I do have something big to tell you, Ginger." I had to get this off my chest to clear my mind.

Ginger's eyes widened, and she leaned forward, ducking behind the counter so nobody could hear us. "I knew it, Margo! I knew something had happened. Are you alright? Tell me!"

I took a long, deep breath. "But you have to promise not to tell anyone, all right?"

"Of course," she said.

I wanted to believe her, but Ginger tended to gossip. People were bound to find out about us eventually, though.

"Well, I sort of went on a date the other night with this guy."

"What's his name? You don't have to give me his last name, but at least his first name."

"I can't, Ginger. We only went on one date, so I'm not ready to tell people who he is yet."

"Oh, come on, Margo! I promise I won't look him up on social media. Well, all right, that's a lie. You know that I will anyway. But what happened that's got you all flustered if it was only dinner?"

"Well," I whispered, "he took me to a costly seafood restaurant, and then one thing lead to another and..."

Ginger's eyes bulged, telling me to keep going.

"I lost my virginity. I mean, I gave a guy my virginity. So, there you have it. I had sex. Finally! And it wasn't as painful as I thought it'd be, either. Actually, I enjoyed it. A lot."

Ginger's hands went to her mouth as she let out a huge gasp but dropped them when people looked up. "Oh my gosh, Margo! There's no way in hell that you are *not* going to tell me the name of the first guy you had sex with!"

I continued to shake my head, though. "No, I really can't Ginger. It's nothing personal, I swear. It's just...private, you know? Right now, I'm not telling anyone."

Ginger crossed her arms, just as she had done at the wedding reception. "Margo, the rules of friendship clearly state that you *have* to tell your best friend who you lost your virginity to."

I cleared my throat, correcting her choice of words.

"Sorry," she continued. "Who you *gave* your virginity to. Look, I've told you everything about me! It's part of bonding or whatever. Please, please tell me the name!"

If it had been any other guy, I would have told Ginger all of the juicy details by now. I would have told her how passionate the sex was and that it was everything I had hoped it would be, plus more. That no matter what comes out of this relationship, I will always remember that night and not have any regrets.

But of course, I couldn't, because it was her big brother, and I was being to suspect she suspected the truth.

"Maybe in time, I will, Ginger, but please accept that I can't tell you. Anyway, that's why my mind's been all over the place today. I just hope that Guadalupe doesn't write me up for what happened with that client. It was an honest mistake."

Ginger rolled her eyes about the client.

"Oh, that bitch? She complains about everybody here. I'm surprised Guadalupe and her husband haven't banned her from the salon yet. But anyway, I'm not going to stop bothering you until you tell me his name."

I just shook my head and leaned back in my chair, making

it clear that I may very well take this to my grave. Besides, Ginger didn't need to know every piece of gossip that happened at the spa. It would serve her right to let this one slide.

"Ginger, if you're really my best friend, then you'll stop asking me. I promise I'll tell you when I'm ready."

She just shook her head as a client walked in through the door.

"Hello, I have an appointment with Margo for a waxing."

Ginger looked at me as I jumped up from my chair, then rushed back into the salon.

As my next client sat down in the chair for facial waxing, Ginger kept her eyes on me. Maybe I shouldn't have even told her about losing my virginity, or perhaps it was a good thing that I wasn't telling her that it was Chase. Regardless, I knew she wouldn't give up on getting the name anytime soon.

By the time I was through working for the day, Ginger had asked me upwards of a dozen times for the name of the guy I had given my virginity to. I'd both had enough, and on some level, I was eager to tell her it was Chase. If he and I were going to keep seeing each other, then she was bound to find out about us anyway.

So we agreed to go to a local cabana for some drinks. I made it clear that I would tell Ginger at the cabana, but not before we got there, and I needed some alcohol in my system. Ginger had a tendency to throw temper tantrums when she didn't get her way, and if she didn't want me dancing with her brother, then she probably wouldn't want me to have sex with him, either.

After our third glass of merlot, Ginger refused to continue to wait.

"It's time, Margo. Tell me his name. You don't have to give me all of the details about how it went down, but as your best friend, I should know who you're having sex with."

I ran my fingers along my empty wine glass, wondering if I should have another one before spilling the beans. But once again, Ginger cleared her throat, signaling that it was time. She was impatient, and I simply couldn't handle the pressure anymore.

"Chase. I gave my virginity to Chase, Ginger."

Her face turned a deep shade of red, and it was evident that she was angry. So angry that she couldn't even find the words to speak.

"Now, I know you're upset, but please hear me out. Chase took me out to a beautiful seafood restaurant, just as I had told you, and then we ended up on the beach. It was just the two of us out there, Ginger, and I can't even begin to describe the magnetic attraction I have to him. I know you're upset, but please don't take it personally."

"I was afraid this would happen." Tears welled in Ginger's eyes, and just as I reached for her hand, she snatched it away and stormed out. Everyone around us turned to see what was going on, and all I could do was sit there dumbfounded.

The bartender came back over to me. "Would you like another drink, miss?"

I shook my head as tears streamed down my face and then threw down some money and hailed a cab.

Sleeping with Chase had turned out to be the worst decision of my life.

12

Chase
Two Weeks Later

It had taken me calling and texting Ginger practically non-stop just to get her to acknowledge my presence. As I sat waiting for her to arrive for lunch at a local soup and sandwich shop, I kept replaying the past two weeks over in my mind.

After Margo gave me her virginity that night on the beach, she had been altogether avoiding me. That was a turn of events I hadn't seen coming. Usually, it was the man who stopped contacting the woman after their first night of sex, but she had yet to pick up any of my phone calls. I had even sent her numerous text messages, wondering if she was simply embarrassed.

But she didn't reply to any of those, either.

I finally succumbed to going to her apartment, where I knocked on her door so loudly that I expected the police to show up. And even though I knew she was home, Margo never answered the door or acknowledged my presence. All I could think of was that it had to do with Ginger.

She had probably told Ginger about our night together, and naturally, my younger sister had flipped out. I'd feel terrible if that were the case because, as her older brother, it's partially my job to make her grow up. But she was about to graduate with her MBA, for crying out loud. If she wasn't mature now, then when would it happen?

Ginger stopped speaking with me almost immediately after my night with Margo. That part I expected, though. Margo and I knew she didn't want us seeing each other, and I knew it would only be a matter of time before she told Ginger that we'd had sex. Naturally, my sister threw a temper tantrum, which is probably why she wouldn't even look at me during any of our weekly family luncheons.

Ginger usually sat right next to me at whatever local restaurant our parents had picked since we'd always been pretty close, but she sat at the opposite end of the table at our last two lunches. Even our parents commented about how uncomfortable and tense the atmosphere had been, but neither one of us said a word about it. We merely shrugged while changing the direction of the conversation.

I couldn't exactly blurt out that I had taken her best friend's virginity, especially in front of our parents.

But I was done with her antics.

I tapped my feet against the table while waiting for Ginger to show up, and when she finally did, I straightened in my chair. She was a grown woman who needed to get it together. I would confront her about the past two weeks and demand to know what her problem was. So what if I'd had sex with her best friend, anyway? How was that any of her business?

Ginger yanked the chair out from the table and sat down, pouting the entire time. Her bottom lip even protruded a little bit. She refused to make eye contact with me as she looked over the beverage section of the menu, even though she always got the same drink.

The waiter came over, and she ordered water without even looking at him, let alone saying "please" or "thank you."

"That's not how our parents raised us, Ginger."

She glared at me from across the table, refusing to say a word. She could have been an ice princess with the way her eyes pierced into my soul.

"What is your deal, anyway? Tell me. Be an adult and just spit it out already, Ginger. It's time for you to grow up, and I mean it this time."

Ginger folded her hands in her lap and leaned across the table. "I can look the other way when you hook up with women, knowing damn well you don't want anything serious, even though you tell them otherwise, but not when you do it to my best friend."

"Now wait a minute—"

"No, Chase. *You* wait a minute. Maybe women are trophies to guys like you, especially when they're a virgin. I know it's just another notch in your belt and being a virgin must have been like winning an Academy Award. But you went too far this time, Chase. You slept with the wrong woman."

"What are you even talking about, Ginger?"

She rolled her eyes at me before continuing her rant. "You know exactly what I'm talking about, Chase. You put Margo in that position. You wined and dined her, and then when she was good and drunk, you just took her virginity. Because that's what guys like you love to do! *You* did this to Margo, Chase. Not me!"

I was done listening to her lies. "I don't know what kind of twisted world you live in, little sister, but Margo gave me full consent for everything that night. Do you really think that I'm such a shitty person that I would just take her virginity and never contact her again?"

Ginger nodded but didn't say a word.

"She and I are two grown-ass adults who consented to everything that happened on that beach. Nothing was done without feelings and meaning, either. And for the record, I do want to keep dating Margo. It wasn't a one-night stand for me. Of course, since you're her best friend, I do want you to be on board with our relationship, but she won't answer or return my calls."

Ginger just shrugged as the waiter returned, where both of us placed our order. After he walked away, I leaned across the table and glared at her.

"Ginger, I want to keep seeing Margo, but only if it's okay with you. You're my little sister, and blood is thicker than water. Please believe me when I say that I genuinely care about her. Was I a jerk and a playboy back in college? Yes, and I regret it...kind of. But people grow up, although you should have grown up a hell of a long time ago. The point is, that Margo is different, Ginger. I want to see her, get to know her, spend time with her. She's not just another woman in a list of names. But I need your blessing."

"You really want to keep seeing Margo, Chase?"

All I could do was nod as I had laid all of my cards out on the table.

"Well, good luck with that."

"What does that even mean, Ginger? 'Good luck with that'?"

All she did was shrug, and we sat in silence for the rest of our meal. The two of us quietly ate our soup and sandwich, although I couldn't bring myself even to pick up my spoon, let alone take a bite of my lunch. My stomach might have been growling, but I was far too upset to eat.

I had finally found happiness after being alone for so long, and my little sister had to get in the way. I couldn't believe she thought so poorly of me. I wasn't the only guy in college who had screwed around, and I knew some women who had acted that way too. It's what you do when you're a young adult. You meet people, fool around, and figure out what you're into sexually.

By the time Ginger had finished with her food, I had

taken all but three sips of my cold soup and a lick of my tomato and basil sandwich. After taking a final sip of her water, she stood up and walked over to me, placing her hand on my shoulder.

"I stand corrected on something, Chase. You are a good man. You do a lot of good things in this world, including donating to charities and showing Margo a good time, but you're not the kind of *good* man that she needs. And there's nothing wrong with that because not everyone is meant to be together in life. I just know both of you too well to know that it won't work, and let me be brutally honest Chase. I refuse to be the one who picks up the pieces."

I glared at her. "What the hell, Ginger?"

"You and I both know that will happen if you pursue Margo, Chase. Something will happen where it just won't work out. The spark will die, you'll find another woman to be with, and then she'll come running to me saying that my brother broke her heart. And then I'll have to hear your side of the story while trying to be empathetic because we're siblings. It'll just be too much for me to handle, Chase. I'm trying hard to pass my exams and graduate. So, as bad as it sounds, I don't have time for any distractions from either you or Margo over this."

The two of us stared at each other for a few moments. On some level, I wondered if Ginger was right. Maybe the spark would die out. But then again, I had never felt this kind of attraction to someone before. It was unlike anything I'd ever experienced.

I went to say something, but Ginger promptly walked away, leaving me alone to stare at my cold soup.

The waiter came by and gave me a concerned look.

"Is there something wrong with your lunch, sir?"

I took a look around the room at all of the happy couples. Men with their arms around their women, laughing and joking while enjoying their meal. That's what I wanted between Margo and me.

"No," I said while giving him my credit card.

Even after I paid the bill, I sat there for a while, wondering if I had screwed everything up. Maybe I should have never pursued Margo after the wedding reception. I could have given her clutch to Ginger, who would have inevitably given it to Margo, and none of this would have happened. I wouldn't be sitting here, staring at cold soup, devastated that both my younger sister and the first woman I had been interested in since Amber were both ignoring me.

But the worst part was that I didn't have a choice in the matter. My attraction to Margo was beyond my control.

13

Margo

Chase banging on my door woke me up from my afternoon nap. I was dreaming about us on the beach again, making love under the full moon as the waves caressed the shore. This time I was on top as we both climaxed, and as he filled me up, he was lavishing my breasts with attention.

Even as I heard him banging, I tried convincing myself that it was part of my dream.

Keep sleeping, Margo. That's not Chase at your door.

Except that his banging became so hard that my walls began to shake, which made me think about how much our bed would shake as we made passionate love every night. Getting over Nick had been trying, and we had never even had sex, and after one date with Chase, I found it impossible to detach myself from him emotionally.

I jumped up off of the couch, running my hands through my hair while trying to figure out what to do. If I let Chase in, we would inevitably end up having sex again, and I would fall head over heels for the guy. But if I didn't acknowledge him, then how much longer would this go on? My heart couldn't keep taking this pain.

"Margo, open up! Please, I need to talk to you!" The desperation in his voice pulled on my heartstrings.

I wanted so badly to tell him that it wasn't me who wanted to keep him away, that it was Ginger. Seeing her walk out on me at the bar was a huge wake-up call. She was my best friend, and the thought of losing her ate me alive. And who was Chase but a guy I had just met who I just happened to give what I had been keeping for that one special guy?

"Please, Margo! Please open up!"

But he wasn't just *any* guy and not just because I had given him my virginity. I had been on dozens of dates before, and eventually, I stopped thinking about the man. But not Chase. I hadn't been able to stop thinking about him ever since I had woken up the next morning.

"Margo, I'm begging you to please open the door!"

I hugged myself as I thought about how good it had felt, making love to Chase. In fact, I wouldn't have changed anything about that night. The setting, the restaurant, and the beach made it all seem too perfect. I had found myself wanting to tell him that I was in love with him, but thankfully

I hadn't. Luckily I had kept that thought inside of me. We had only just met, and you didn't have to be in love with someone to have sex.

In a perfect world, Chase and I could be together without any repercussions. But we didn't live in a perfect world, and not only was she my best friend, but I worked with her. Every day I saw her, and every day she refused to make eye contact with me before she rushed out the door to study or finish an assignment. Ginger had no time for me. It killed me inside. I'd even tried telling her that our attraction was beyond our control, but all she did was wave me goodbye.

She didn't want to hear anything that I had to say.

For someone who desperately needed the attention of a man, Ginger sure was judgmental about my dating her brother. But she didn't see it that way, of course. She was always telling me that I could have any guy I wanted, but that was just it. I didn't want just *any* man. I found most men revolting and only after one thing, but not Chase. That must have been what I picked up on the first night we had met.

In addition to our intense sexual chemistry, he was a guy who wanted more than a one-night stand. The exact type of man I had been waiting to give my virginity to for far too long.

Every time Chase had come knocking on my door, all I could do was fight the tears as they poured down my face, wanting nothing more than to tell him why we couldn't see each other anymore. I could tell him precisely what Ginger had done that night at the cabana, and of course, he would fully understand. Even as a guy, he was sure to understand just how meaningful female relationships were to women.

By that point, I knew that my neighbors had heard him screaming for me, which ate me up inside even more so. I couldn't be that mad at Ginger, either. Maybe she knew something about Chase that I didn't, or perhaps it really did come down to jealousy. What did I know about having brothers, anyway?

I had been an only child.

I buried my face in my hands as he continued to bang on the door, desperately pleading with me to open it. And God, how I wanted to. Just to see his face staring back at me, the way he had done so on the beach that night underneath the stars. And I could never forget the moment that he accepted my virginity. Everyone had said that it was painful, but not with Chase. He had been gentle and patient. He hadn't rushed anything or treated my body and the gift I gave him with anything but respect, and I had loved every minute of our time together. In fact, it was the most pleasurable experience of my life.

"Margo, please. I'll do anything! Anything, just let me in so we can talk!"

I kept shaking my head while crying even harder. Ginger would be livid if she knew he was at my apartment at that moment, banging on my door. She would be upset if she knew that I still wanted him. After getting up and walking out on me that night, the air between us had been so tense and uncomfortable at the spa. I wanted everything to go back to normal.

I was torn between a man I couldn't stay away from and my best friend.

Chase's knocks started to get even louder, pulling me out of my trance.

If I didn't put an end to this madness now, then it would only get worse. Chase would keep coming by at all hours of the day and night, pounding away at my door between calling and texting me. And every time he did it, another part of me died inside.

But I froze as my hand reached the doorknob. How could I look Chase in the face, tell him to leave, and delete my number? How could I have waited all of that time to have sex, only to say to a guy that clearly wanted to be with me that I wanted nothing to do with him?

The answer was clear—I couldn't.

I slowly ran my fingers over the doorknob as he continued to knock, but something told me he knew I was directly on the other side. He must have heard my footsteps in the hallway and knew I was getting close to letting him in. I finally grabbed the handle, and after a few more knocks from him, I decided to get it over with.

I flipped the lock and whipped open the door, my face strewn with tears as I still wasn't sure what I was going to say. But as I was about to speak, Chase grabbed my cheeks and kissed me. He ran his fingers through my hair as our tongues made love to each other and we made our way inside. I used my foot to slam the door shut, not wanting my nosy neighbor across the hall to see us.

Although, I was sure she had been watching through her peephole.

By the time we made it into my bedroom, I knew I could never tell him to leave me alone.

Chase and I started ripping off our clothes, but only down to our underwear. His muscles pushed against my skin as we toppled onto my bed, and I wrapped my legs around him as he kissed me passionately. As much as I wanted him inside of me, I was more concerned with just having him in my arms again, feeling his strong, masculine touch enveloping me after being away from each other for far too long.

When Chase rolled us over, I landed on top, straddling his waist. But before I could go any further, Chase leaned up on his elbows and stared into my eyes. "Margo, is this what you want? Do you really want this between us? And I don't just mean tonight."

Instead of responding, I slid down his legs, slid my fingers underneath his boxer shorts, and felt the tip of his hardness. I leaned back on my knees, searching his face before I could come up with an answer. Chase was asking me to be more than just someone he has great sex with. He wanted to know if we would go forward with this, date each other, and see where it leads. It would only tarnish my relationship with Ginger, but I wasn't in control of my emotions anymore.

Not since that night on the beach.

I nodded, doing my best to reassure him that it was, without a doubt, what I wanted.

That wasn't enough for Chase, though. "No, Margo. I need to hear you say the words."

After clearing the lump in my throat, I replied, "Yes, Chase. This is something that I want."

Chase sat up, grabbed me for a kiss, and then he slid his boxers off until they were on my floor, followed by my red, satin panties. Fully divested of all our clothing, I situated myself on his waist and held his eyes as I slid his shaft inside of me. The intimacy of that stare was more potent than the connection between our two bodies. It was raw but full of passion, and oh God, it felt good.

Both of us moaned so loud that I was sure we disturbed some neighbors. I bucked back and forth as I rode him for the first time, encouraging him to push as far into me as possible. I loved the look of pure ecstasy on his face as his mouth went slack each time I squeezed his cock with my muscles or found a move that hit him just right.

Chase's strong, masculine hands ran up and down my body, feeling my soft skin and then rubbing my clit. I loved that he could watch me enjoy the feel of him inside me and being on top gave Chase the freedom to use his hands to explore my body. He took full advantage until we'd both reached that apex together. That high was more beautiful and exquisite than anything I'd ever experienced, and I wondered if I'd feel that same sense of wonder and satisfaction every time Chase made love to me.

Once we caught our breaths and he had his arm around me again, he kissed the top of my head and caressed my arm. "I meant what I said, you know, about us seeing each other more often."

I traced his erect nipple with my finger. "Oh, I know. And I want to see you, too. I'm sorry for...everything. It has to do with Ginger."

"I figured," he said with a sigh. "We'll discuss that another time, but I'd like to take you out again."

I briefly wondered what Ginger would say about us getting together, then remembered that at this point, it didn't really matter. I had already committed myself to Chase.

"That sounds great. Where do you want to go?"

"I'm thinking about dinner and a movie. A perfect date."

"That sounds lovely, Chase."

And as the two of us fell asleep, I accepted the fact that I might lose Ginger over this relationship. And I decided that was a risk I was willing to take.

14

Chase

After a nap and a long, semi-tearful goodbye with Margo, I left her place and decided to walk down to the nearest cabana. Our passionate love-making session was just what I needed after the living hell of those past two weeks, and I wanted to celebrate. The one just down the road from her place made the best Spiced Apple Sangria I had ever tasted.

It was usually sunny in Miami Beach, but it felt even brighter today. Before I had met Margo, the only woman I had ever been that obsessed with was Amber. After that relationship had ended, I never thought that I'd feel that way about another woman. But no matter what I did, something kept pulling me back to Margo. I had never been the type of guy who bangs on a door, demanding the woman open up, but I had no control over this relationship.

My emotions ran the show.

As soon as I took a left after leaving her building on foot, Ginger came around the corner and nearly crashed right into me.

You have got to be kidding me!

Her eyes widened farther than I had ever seen before, and her slightly tanned face was getting darker with every passing second. I had to come up with a lie about why I was at Margo's apartment complex, but I couldn't formulate anything believable in the seconds before Ginger spoke. It wasn't long before her hands at her sides turned into fists, and just as I was about to open my mouth, she tore right into me.

"I knew it, Chase Bowers! I knew you couldn't stay away from Margo!"

"No," I said while putting my hands up in defense, "please hear me out before—"

"Absolutely not! I don't want to listen to anything you have to say to me, you idiot! Even after I made it clear that you two *cannot* date each other, here you are, walking away after you probably just had sex!"

I exhaled deeply while running my hands through my hair, feeling defenseless and stumped. Obviously, I was coming from Margo's apartment—who else would I be there to see? I contemplated telling her that Margo had left something in my car, but nothing got past my sister.

So, I decided to be honest with her.

"First of all, what two consenting adults do behind closed—"

"Consenting my ass, Chase! I know how you are with women. I've seen it firsthand. You picked up on her innocence the second you laid eyes on her, didn't you?"

What the hell are you talking about?

"Ginger, no! For crying out loud, I'm not some predator—"

"Stop lying to me, Chase. You might be a good man on some level, but as I said to you over lunch, you are *not* the man for Margo! She's my best friend, and I know what the hell I'm talking about! I've seen the way you've treated other women."

"Okay, yes, I've been a bit of a playboy in the past, but I've changed! Seriously, Ginger. I'm a grown man!"

She let out a disgusted sigh.

"Maybe things really are different between you and Margo, as opposed to other women. But you two aren't a good match. The flame between you two will inevitably fade, and when everything falls apart, I'll be the one to clean up the mess!"

I rolled my eyes at her, desperate to get through her hard head. "Oh, get off of your high horse, Ginger! Not once have I ever needed you to clean up my mess, and none of this is about *you*."

"Oh please, Chase. You've cried on my shoulders far too many times, and quite frankly, I'm tired of it being drenched with your tears! I'm not doing this anymore! I'm not a trained therapist, you know!" She was delusional.

I snickered directly into her face. "Not once have I *ever* cried on your shoulder, Ginger! Perhaps you're forgetting who you're dealing with. I'm Chase Bowers, a billionaire tech titan who can do just fine standing on his own two feet. Crying on your shoulder, my ass!"

Ginger folded her arms while glaring at me, and I caught the faintest glimmer of a smile. "Perhaps you've forgotten about all of those three o'clock in the morning phone calls, right after Amber up and walked out on you. You remember those calls, right Chase? The nights when you couldn't sleep because the bed was cold and empty, and you knew she was with another man. Isn't that right, Chase?"

Ginger knew what she was doing. She knew Amber was an incredibly sore subject for me.

"Excuse me?"

She snickered in such a way that I wanted to scream. "Don't act so stupid, Chase. How many times did I tell you that Amber would leave you for her high school sweetheart? And yet you refused to break-up with her, even going so far as to let her move in! It's your own damn fault that she married him too. And I'm sure you've seen their honeymoon photos on Instagram."

Now it was my hands that were forming fists at my side. "You just sunk to a new low, Ginger. You know damn well that mentioning Amber is off-limits!"

"Off-limits? You want to talk about off-limits? Then stay the hell away from Margo before it's too late, or I guarantee that we'll have another Amber situation on our hands. But guess what, Chase? I won't be answering your three o'clock phone calls. Not from you and not from Margo. Because I am done!"

I started to pace back and forth, ignoring the stares from people getting out of their cars. Thankfully, the parking lot wasn't too full, though.

"So what are you saying, Ginger? Are you actually saying that if I choose to keep dating Margo that you're going to break-off all communications with me? Just shut your own damn brother out of your life?"

She didn't answer my question, though. Ginger just leaned up against the building, staring at me as her faint smile started to widen.

"Going forward, dear sister, don't you *ever* bring up Amber's name again. That was a completely different situation than what I currently have with Margo."

"Oh please, Chase. You haven't changed *that* much. I know exactly how all of this will unfold too. You just can't see it yet. It's no different than Amber."

All I could do was stand there, in front of my sister, wondering what to say next. She wasn't wrong about those late-night phone calls after Amber had left me, but things were much different this time around. The connection between us was unlike anything I had ever experienced. I couldn't go to sleep without thinking about Margo, let alone focus on anything related to work.

"You have it all wrong, Ginger. Amber is in the past, and going forward, I forbid you from bringing up her name. Do you understand me? Don't you ever mention Amber again, much less in reference to Margo!"

Once again, she snickered at me, right as the wind blew her hair, causing it to cover part of her face. For several minutes, all I could see were her angry eyes piercing into mine.

"Apparently, it needs to be brought up because here we are again Chase. We're right back to square one, except this time you're doing it with my best friend. So if you think that I've sunk to a new low, take a look in the mirror."

Ginger and I'd had numerous fights over the years, as siblings often do, but nothing was nearly as intense as this one. I had never seen her so angry and defiant before. She had always been a drama queen, but this was a side that had never reared its ugly head until that moment.

When I refused to speak, Ginger stepped a little bit closer and cleared her throat.

"I meant every word of what I said, Chase. If you continue to see Margo, then don't come crying to me when everything ends. I just can't believe I actually thought you two could stay away from each other. Do you realize how foolish you've made me look?"

"For the millionth time, Ginger, this isn't about you! Why are you such a self-centered little brat? Stop acting as though the world revolves around you. All that you're doing is hurting your best friend with this nonsense and me! You're a grown-ass woman who, *hello*, is about to earn her MBA! Do you really think this is acceptable behavior for someone your age?"

She rolled her eyes while throwing her hands into the air toward me.

"You're one to talk, Chase. Just admit that you're scratching an itch with Margo, and eventually, it'll end. Look me in the eyes and tell me I'm wrong, Chase. Now."

I'd had enough.

I flung my hands up into the air, leaned into her face, and screamed, "Fine! You want me to stop seeing Margo? Is that what you want?"

Ginger's smug smile filled me with rage. "Yes, that's exactly what I want."

I leaned even closer to her face before screaming this time. "Well, you don't get to dictate that about my life or your best friend's!"

Ginger's mouth dropped, shocked at my refusal to stop dating Margo. She looked as though I'd slapped her, and I knew there was no coming back from what I had just done. There was nothing that I could possibly say to fix our relationship—as brother and sister—at that point, and I genuinely didn't care.

As she stood there on the sidewalk, realizing she was defeated, I stormed past her and made my way home. All I wanted to do was call Margo. I needed to hear her voice again, even though I had just left her apartment. After everything I had gone through in my life—my businesses, a failed relationship with Amber, outgrowing my playboy ways—nothing had felt more right than being with Margo. There was no way in hell I was giving it up because Ginger had a hair up her ass and couldn't stand not being the center of attention.

Margo was everything that I had ever wanted in a romantic partner. Or dare I say, soulmate. And nothing could get in my way. In fact, just knowing Ginger was so against us being together made me want to be with Margo even more. So she could throw all of the temper tantrums she wished to about us, but come hell or high water, my sister wouldn't keep me from that amazing woman.

15

Margo
Five Weeks Later

As soon as my last client of the day paid, I did a half-ass job of cleaning up my workstation and then made a beeline for the bathroom. It had taken everything inside of me not to pass out while applying my client's makeup. With my face just a few inches away from hers, I hoped she didn't hear my stomach gurgling as I had applied a second coat of mascara.

The past week at the spa had been a complete nightmare. Every day I woke up with a headache and stomach cramps, and the only thing that took care of it was sleeping. I had almost called in sick to work that morning too. I woke up with what I could only describe as a migraine, took some pain pills on an empty stomach, and then did the bare minimum to make myself appear presentable.

Everyone at the spa kept staring at me.

A few of the other girls at work asked if I was feeling okay, to which I simply nodded. The less noise for me, the better. Even the clicking of high heels on the floor felt like nails hammered into my head, and any smell made me nauseous. I sipped on ginger ale throughout the day, hoping it would make it feel better, but that only gave me the hiccups between unladylike belching.

I had no idea what I was doing in the bathroom. I just needed to be alone for a few minutes to try to figure out what was wrong with me and take a breather from the bustle of the spa. Thankfully, it was a one-stall bathroom, so nobody would walk in and see me hovering over the sink. I splashed some cold water onto my face, hoping to help with the headache, but it did absolutely nothing. After drinking several small cups of water, I made my way out of the bathroom and decided to hit up the pharmacy. There had to be some type of over-the-counter medication I could take to at least help with my stomach.

The traffic in Miami Beach was bumper-to-bumper, and the only relief I found was leaning back while driving with my arms straight forward. Everyone around me was honking their horns, which amplified my pounding head and threatening stomach. I wanted to scream at them to shut up, but that would only add to the noise and irritate me more.

By the time I pulled into the parking lot, the pharmacy was closed.

Why aren't they twenty-four hours like everywhere else?

I whipped out my cellphone and called Guadalupe at home, who answered on the first ring.

"Hello, darling! How was work today?"

"Everything went well with the clients, but I've been sick all week."

"Oh no," she cried into the phone. "What's wrong with you?"

I rubbed my stomach with my left hand while talking into the speakerphone. "I've had a headache and stomach cramps all week, and the only thing that helps is sleep. But obviously, I can't sleep all day, and now the pharmacy is closed. I'll do anything to feel better at this point!"

"Come to my house, dear. I have something that'll make you feel better."

By the time I pulled into Guadalupe's driveway, all I wanted to do was lay down and fall asleep. She opened the front door as soon as my heels hit her steps and greeted me with her usual warm hug.

"Thank you," I said while making my way into her home. She hadn't even done anything, but just being around her made me feel cared for.

Pineapple knick-knacks, paintings of the ocean, and several religious statues decorated the quaint space. She guided me over to her oversized white couch, which I gladly let myself sink into.

"Just wait right here," she said while placing a pillow behind my neck, "and I'll be back."

When Guadalupe returned less than a minute later, she carried a cup of hot herbal tea on a saucer. I took it from her and sipped it slowly, praying the herbs would make my aches and pains go away.

"I hope this helps, Guadalupe."

She ran one hand through my hair while rubbing my thigh with the other. "You poor thing. I wish you had said something to me sooner. Maybe we could have had one of the other ladies help you out at the spa."

"That's all right," I said, blowing on the tea. "I can't afford to call in sick, and I wouldn't want to put that on the other girls anyway."

"I don't want you thinking that way, dear. We are one big family down at the spa. Are you enjoying life in a big city? It must be very different from where you grew up."

"I love it here, Guadalupe. And I'm surprised by how friendly everyone is in Miami Beach. It must be the constant sunshine."

She kept running her hand through my hair while smiling. "Life in a big city is simply more fast-paced, and how can anyone be upset when the sun is always shining?" Guadalupe paused for a few moments, during which time the only sound was of me sipping the delicious herbal tea. "Now, what is his name and how long have you been dating him?"

The antique teacup and saucer just about fell out of my hand. "Um, what are you talking about?"

Guadalupe kissed my forehead as I drank the rest of the tea, eager to get all of the herbs inside of my body. "This guy you're dating. I want to know all about him."

I set the teacup and saucer onto her coffee table, wondering how she knew about Chase and me. But then I remembered that nothing got past Guadalupe. "Well, his name is Chase Bowers, and we've been dating for a little over a month now. He's in the technology industry, although I've heard people refer to him as a 'tech titan.' Whatever that means. Anyway, we met at a wedding a little over a month ago and, well, he's amazing. I've never had these feelings for another guy."

Guadalupe's eyes started to widen, and I knew what her next words would be. "Is he alto, oscuro y guapo, Margo? Oh, please tell me he is, darling!"

As the herbal tea started to take care of both my stomach and head, I giggled while nodding at her. "Yes, Guadalupe. He's very much the tall, dark, and handsome type."

She nearly jumped off the couch while clapping her hands together, which made me laugh even harder. Guadalupe loved to live vicariously through her female employees. "Oh, this is wonderful! You know, Margo, you *always* keep a tall, dark, and handsome man! Now, I have some ideas for the wedding. Since we're in Miami Beach, you'll probably want to go with a beach theme. And you have the perfect body for a strapless wedding dress! Oh, I can bake the cake for it too! Did I tell you that I used to make wedding cakes?"

I couldn't listen to her get excited about Chase anymore,

though. “No, you didn’t, but our relationship isn’t as great as you might think, Guadalupe.” She leaned back on the couch, clutched her bosom, and gasped. “A few weeks ago, after Chase left my apartment, he ran into Ginger on the sidewalk.”

“Wait, you mean our receptionist, Ginger?”

I nodded while rubbing my stomach. “Yes. Chase is Ginger’s older brother. Anyway, Ginger hasn’t wanted us to be together ever since we met at the wedding, where he went as her date. And I overheard them yelling at each other on the sidewalk, right outside of my window.”

“Oh no,” Guadalupe said while continuing to clutch her bosom. “That’s awful! What did they say, Margo?”

“Ginger laid into him, screaming that she wasn’t going to be there to pick up the pieces when our relationship ended. She said something about his ex-girlfriend, Amber, and how Chase called Ginger crying at three in the morning after Amber left him. It tore me up inside to hear them screaming at each other like that.”

She went back to running her hand through my hair. “Siblings have argued over worse things in life, Margo. You have to follow your intuition, even if it means upsetting Ginger. She’s a sweet young lady, but she should want to see her brother and best friend together.”

I let out a massive sigh before telling her the worst part. “Chase actually said to her, ‘Fine! You want me to stop seeing Margo? Is that what you want?’”

“Oh, no! And what did Ginger say back?”

Tears started to run down my face. "She said, 'Yes, that's exactly what I want.'"

I was sobbing uncontrollably at that point, and Guadalupe leaned forward to kiss me on my forehead.

"Darling, Ginger is wrong in this case. You can't let her dictate what either of you do. What did he say back to her?"

I just shook my head while crying into my hands. "I couldn't keep listening to them, Guadalupe, so I slammed my window shut. But you heard what he asked her. Just hearing him say those words turned me into an emotional wreck!"

After crying for several minutes, I finally composed myself enough to look her in the face. She took my hand and rubbed it, and I was so thankful to have someone like her in my life.

"Only you can decide what's best for your life, Margo. And if this man is what's best for you right now, then you shouldn't let anyone take that away from you. The only power people have over you is the power that you give. You are much stronger than you realize, dear. That's one of the reasons I hired you."

I searched her eyes as she continued to rub my hand.

"Are you serious, Guadalupe? I thought you hired me because of my license."

My comment made her chuckle.

"Having a license in your work line is necessary, yes, but I'm a good judge of character, Margo. The way you held yourself during the interview told me you were reliable. And you haven't let me down yet."

Her words pulled at my heartstrings. Even before I

became sick, there were times when I struggled to keep up with such a rigorous work schedule. Just knowing that she had faith in me started to make me feel better.

"Thank you, Guadalupe. That means so much to me."

"So please, take back control over your life. Don't let Ginger or anyone else keep you from being with Chase, all right?"

I nodded while giving her my best smile. "All right, Guadalupe. I won't."

She patted my knee while standing up.

"Oh, and you need to come with me." She held out her hand to me, which I took even though I didn't know where we were going. "We need to get you a pregnancy test, dear."

My mouth fell open as she continued to hold my hand. All I could do was stare at her as if she had suddenly grown an extra pair of eyes. Then I finally found the courage to speak. "What...what did you say?"

"Come on, dear. You need to take a pregnancy test."

"Why in the world do you have pregnancy tests on hand?"

Guadalupe simply laughed as she pulled me up from my seat, refusing to let it go as we walked further into her house.

16

Chase

It had been a long flight, and despite sitting in a comfortable first-class seat, I was beyond antsy. My leg didn't stop tapping the entire fourteen-hour flight back to Key Biscayne, which I usually would have taken the time to enjoy. Before meeting Margo, I never wanted my trips to end because it meant going home to an empty house. The longer I was up in the air, the longer it would be until loneliness paid me an unwanted visit.

But as we gently flew over the Atlantic Ocean, I found myself staring at my cellphone more than the jaw-dropping view below.

Margo hadn't been answering my text messages for quite some time. She had always had her "read receipt" option on.

So as soon as she opened the message, I received an alert on my phone. It was a feature I appreciated, but not many people used. She also hadn't been answering any of my calls. I even made sure to call her when I knew she wasn't working, and each time I left her a voicemail, begging that she get back to me.

Margo had yet to do that, either, though.

Once again, I was forced to go over to her apartment complex on multiple occasions, where I ruthlessly banged on her front door, begging and pleading for her to open it. I couldn't believe I had let a woman bring me to my knees, but I had completely lost control of my emotions. Margo had taken up permanent space in my mind, where images of her smiling back at me were on constant replay.

This was worse than when Amber had walked out on me.

Refusing to give up on what I knew to be a sure thing, I sent her one more text message before my flight landed.

Chase: Margo, I know this has something to do with Ginger. Whatever she said or did to you, please forget it. You and I both know we're meant to be together. I can't stop thinking about you, and I refuse to give up on us. Please, at least open up this message, so I know you received it. I'm begging you.

I hit the "send" button and then threw my phone back into my briefcase, knowing damn well that she wouldn't respond.

As I stared out the window, forcing myself to enjoy the

view as we got closer to landing, I found myself getting angry. Not at Margo, though.

I was furious with my sister.

I knew damn well that she was behind the Margo situation. She had done nothing but make a mess of things from the word go, and she had something to do with Margo refusing to read my text messages, answer any of my phone calls, and reply to my voicemails. Once again, my spoiled little brat of a sister had gotten her way by throwing a temper tantrum. But unlike other ones she'd had thrown, where the family and I just let her have her way, I wasn't going to let her win this time.

As soon as the plane landed back home after my latest business trip, I would head directly to Ginger's place and confront her. If she thought she could get away with ruining my life, then she had another think coming.

By the time my plane landed, I had spent far too much time contemplating how Ginger had gone too far this time. Even my driver had given me a concerned look, especially when I practically barked out my sister's address.

I pounded on Ginger's front door more aggressively than I did at Margo's, and her voice came roaring through.

"Hang on a second, gosh! I literally just got out of the shower, Chase."

"Open this door right now, Ginger! You've gone too far this time."

It took her a good ten minutes to finally make an appearance.

"Chase, what's wrong? Why are you pounding on my door, and what are you talking about that I've 'gone too far'?"

"What's *wrong*? I'll tell you what's *wrong*! You got into Margo's head so bad with your nonsense that she won't even open up a damn text message from me! What the hell did you say to her that I can't even get a read receipt back?"

Ginger leaned back her head as she placed her palm onto her chest, shocked that I would accuse her of doing such a thing. It was just more drama from the queen. "Okay, first of all, you need to kick it—"

I barged my way into her apartment, then marched into her living room, where I began to pace back and forth. Ginger just stood in the entryway, watching me with a bewildered look on her face as my face turned red with anger.

"I don't 'need' to do anything, Ginger! You've gone too far this time. What the hell are you even saying to her at work? Huh? Are you telling her that it's only a matter of time before I cheat on her, or are you saying that she deserves a better man? Yes, you have had to comfort a few of my ex-girlfriends after I broke their hearts, but how many times do I have to tell you that it's different between Margo and me?"

"Chase, before you continue can I just—"

"No," I shouted. "No more 'saying' anything, Ginger! God, you are an incredibly selfish and insane human being! In what world do you live in that you think any of this is okay? So your best friend is dating your older brother? Why is that such a big deal? Even you admitted that I *am* a good man!"

She leaned against the entryway, folding her arms across her chest, raising her brow. "If you'll just let me say that—"

"Are you telling Margo that it's only a matter of time before she's crying on your shoulder, wondering why you let her get close to me? Or maybe you're telling her that I treat women like property and that she's just another notch in my belt?"

"Chase Bowers, if you'll just let me—"

I threw my hands up into the air, not allowing my little sister to get in a word. "What gets me the most, Ginger, is that we've always been so close. All of those times when you needed help while in college, be it to cover a few bills or a place to stay while you found a cheaper place to live. And what about all of the stuff I did for you when you were in high school, covering your ass while you were dating guys behind Mom and Dad's back? Taking you to the prom—for the love of God, Ginger, I bend over backward for you. I swear I have never known a more selfish person!"

Ginger pushed off the wall she'd been leaning on, furrowed her brow, and put her hands on her hips, undoubtedly on the verge of unleashing one of her temper tantrums.

"You're not fair to me at all, Chase! Please—"

"Fair? You wanna talk about fair? I'm not the same man I was ten years ago. Hell, I'm not even the same guy from a year ago! I'm not going to break Margo's heart! Do you honestly think that I would be banging on her door, demanding that she speak to me if I didn't have genuine feelings for her? No man in this world would act that way toward someone if all they were after were sex. I can get laid anywhere."

Ginger continued to stand in the doorway, shaking her head back and forth.

"If you'd let me speak, then you'd know that I haven't seen or heard from Margo in a week, Chase!"

A lump formed in my throat, as I suddenly realized what that meant. "Wait, why hasn't she been at work all week?"

Ginger shrugged, clearly as perplexed as me. "Apparently, she put in for some vacation time, but she hasn't been there long enough to have any vacation time. We don't get any for the first year."

I ran my hands through my hair, suddenly worried about what was wrong with Margo. She didn't seem like the type of person who would just go into hiding without telling someone.

As I made my way past Ginger and toward the door, she began to speak again.

"Wait, Chase! Where are you going? When's the last time you heard from her? Chase, get back here!"

By the time I made it out to my car, Ginger's questions had toned down to a low muffle. Even if I owed her an apology for barging in on her like that, she had put me through enough hell to wait. Margo was my biggest concern right now. The two of us might not have known each other for too long, but I knew her well enough to sense that something wasn't right.

As soon as my driver got back into his seat, I rattled off

Margo's address and asked him to go as fast as possible. "If you get pulled over for speeding, I'll have my lawyer expunge it from your record somehow."

He nodded while weaving in and out of traffic with ease, pulling into Margo's driveway right as the sun was starting to set. I jumped out and raced up to her door, where once again, my fists made short work of the wood.

"Margo, I know you're in there, so please open up! I'm begging you! Just open the door so we can talk about this, I need to see you!"

The door handle started to turn, and I stepped back as my heart started racing a mile a minute. I had never felt so much anxiety wash over me at once.

Finally!

When the door finally opened, an elderly Cuban man was smiling back at me. "Good evening, I'm Yuslan, Guadalupe's husband. You must be Chase."

I shook his extended hand, then immediately noticed a large black bag at his side. It wasn't zipped yet, and I could see some bras and panties peeking out.

"You're taking that to Margo, aren't you?"

Yuslan continued to smile at me while holding the bag. "A man is only worth his weight in salt if at first, he grinds himself down into it."

What the hell is this guy talking about?

Yuslan put his hand on my right arm before proceeding to speak. "Sometimes, all you need to do is give a woman a bit of time, even if that does grind your gears."

I was still confused about what the hell Yuslan was talking about, plus I was in no mood for mind games. "Look, I'm worried about Margo, and I need to see her. Please."

Yuslan nodded and gave me a wink. "That's a good place to start, Chase." Yuslan put down the bag, reached over to a table in the hallway, and scribbled down an address on a piece of paper.

He didn't say a word as he slipped it to me either.

17

Margo

The guest bedroom at Guadalupe and Yuslan's home was gorgeous. It was decorated in light pink and lime green, which brought out the beautiful flowers directly outside of the big window. It also had a California king-sized bed with large, fluffy pillows, and sheets with a thread count higher than my budget could ever afford. They also brought in fresh flowers every day and placed them on the bedside table.

It was the same bedside table whose drawer contained my positive pregnancy test.

I pulled it out just as a warm breeze entered through the open window and stared at the double pink lines yet again. There was no denying that I would have Chase's baby.

Between the positive pregnancy test and all of my physical ailments, I was definitely with child.

I shoved it back inside of the drawer, then lay back down on top of the bed. Guadalupe and Yuslan had been letting me stay with them while I tried to process everything, and I kept waiting for something to jolt me out of my trance. I didn't know what I was going to do, and there were moments when I was still in shock.

Am I really pregnant? Is this really happening to me? Will I ever see Chase again?

I hadn't even been at the spa for a year, which meant I was still building up my clientele. I also lived in a tiny, one-bedroom apartment. It was beautiful and had breathtaking views, but it certainly wasn't conducive to raising a child. And there was the fact that I would probably end up being a single mother.

Right before moving to Miami Beach, I had a game plan for how my life would play out: I would build up my clientele and reputation at the spa, meet a man, fall in love, get married, and then start a family. That's what normal people do.

Normal people don't get pregnant by a man they barely even know.

I rolled over and closed my eyes, hoping a short nap would snap me back into reality. But as I started to doze off, all I could think about was Chase. Tall, dark, and handsome Chase, standing in front of me in head-to-toe black, handing me a rose. I dreamed that we walked along the beach again, to the spot where we had made love for the very first time.

It was the spot where I gave him my virginity.

As we started rolling around in the dream, my hand drifted down and rubbed my swollen clit. My fingers went to work as I pictured Chase on top of me, sliding off my silk dress and my dripping-wet panties. I dreamed that his engorged cock found my moist pussy, and as he entered me, so did my fingers in reality.

My back arched in my sleep as he buried himself inside of me, thrusting into me while sucking my nipples.

God, how I loved his attention.

His hands roamed all over my body as we became one, making love under the full moon once again. Even though it was my fingers inside my core instead of his cock, I could feel his thick, long, swollen member in my dream. With every thrust, I pushed myself closer and closer to the edge until finally, both of us climaxed at the exact moment.

I clasped my hand over my mouth as I came, hoping that neither Guadalupe nor Yuslan heard me. It was never my intention to pleasure myself in their guest bedroom, but I couldn't help it. Chase was all I could think about lately, so of course, I'd dream about him.

And gosh, how I so badly wanted to feel him inside of me yet again.

My eyes opened up right after I climaxed.

I need a shower.

After taking a quick shower in the attached guest bathroom, I lay back down on the bed right as Guadalupe knocked on the door.

"Come on in," I said.

She was carrying a large tray that contained tea for two and an assortment of her delicious, homemade pastries.

"I hope you're hungry, dear, because I need an excuse to eat something sweet and share a moment together with you."

Guadalupe set the tray on the edge of the bed and then poured some tea. I sank my teeth into one of her pastries, and it was like tasting a piece of heaven.

"You're going to spoil me with these treats, Guadalupe."

She waved her hand in front of her face and winked. "Are you kidding me? When you're pregnant, you have the best excuse for indulging in desserts. So take advantage while you can! How are you feeling, by the way?"

I took a long sip of her tea, allowing the herbs to make me feel better as they always did. "I don't know what to do, Guadalupe."

She put her hand on my thigh, rubbing it for emotional support. "The only thing you can do is the most you can do."

I smiled and nodded, once again thankful that she was in my life. She and Yuslan were full of wisdom, and I was in desperate need of their little sayings right at that moment. Even when I was feeling as blue as possible, their words of wisdom always made me smile.

"I just keep thinking about him, Guadalupe. Chase. Aside from being alto, oscuro y guapo," she chuckled, "the connection between us is unlike anything that I've ever felt. I just can't see spending the rest of my life without him in it, especially since I'm carrying his child."

Thinking about raising the baby without Chase, its father, was enough to send me over the edge. I started crying directly into my herbal tea, causing some of it to slop out and cover the rest of my half-eaten pastry.

Once again, Guadalupe was there for me.

"Darling, please don't worry so much. Everything has a way of working itself out. Plus, when you're pregnant, stress is horrible for your body."

I looked up at her and nodded, all the while drying my tears.

"I know it's just hard sometimes. If only Ginger weren't his sister, then maybe everything would be different. But it's not, and I still can't believe I got mixed up with her older brother. And not just mixed up, but pregnant! You should have seen the way she glared at the two of us dancing at the wedding. I can't imagine how she'll look at me when she finds out that I'm carrying his child." I started to cry again, but this time, Guadalupe didn't stop me; she understood that when a woman needed to cry, you let her cry.

"It must be very hard on you, dear. I've seen the way you and Ginger are with each other at the spa. It's as clear as day that you two are very close."

I nodded, thinking about all of the good times she and I had shared. "I miss Ginger so much. She's like the sister I never had, and even though she's a bit of a drama queen at times, she's the person I turn to when I need comforting."

"It sounds as though you two are destined for a great friendship, then."

"Yes, we definitely were."

Guadalupe leaned closer to me on the bed. "You feel guilty about something, Margo. Tell me."

It was unbelievable how Guadalupe could instantly know what I was thinking.

I let out a big sigh before looking her right in the eyes. "I feel guilty for missing Chase. There, I said it. I hate that I miss him so much, but I do. I think about him all the time, and I hate the position Ginger's feelings have put all three of us in."

"Margo, you know that Yuslan and I have been married for a long time. I've had to give him multiple second chances over the years because that's what you do in a relationship. People have this thwarted idea that relationships and marriage are supposed to be perfect, that the less you fight, the more compatible you are. That's hogwash."

Seeing her get so worked up made me giggle. "Really? You two have had problems?"

Guadalupe rolled her eyes while placing the back of her palm on her forehead. "During the first few years of our marriage, Yuslan repeatedly forgot both our wedding anniversary and my birthday. Even though I never forgot his. My mother kept telling me to divorce him, because if he really loved me, then he wouldn't have forgotten. Well, I knew better. So I decided to forget *his* birthday one year. Now keep in mind that I always baked him a cake and threw an elaborate party."

"How did he respond?"

"Yuslan never forgot another one of my birthdays or our wedding anniversary. What I'm about to say might come as a shock to you, Margo. While neither one of us has never cheated, we have flirted with the opposite sex."

I chuckled while nodding, thinking about how she flirted with younger men who were tall, dark, and handsome.

"Anyway," she continued, "it's a form of respect not to do it in front of your spouse. One night, Yuslan and I were out to dinner, and he kept flirting with the waitress. He didn't mean anything by it, but it was still inappropriate, and it hurt my feelings."

"What did you do?"

"I flirted with a man at the salon right in front of him the next day! And guess what? He hasn't done it since. Now, I should also point out that he apologized profusely after each of these instances. But my point is that you have to give people second chances, Margo. And sometimes third, fourth, fifth—you see where I'm going, right?"

I nodded while eating the rest of my pastry.

"Remember, Margo: it's not about the number of chances you give, it's about the number of times you reach for each other and strive to do better."

"I see what you're saying," I said. "And I think it's time that I finally call Chase."

"Before you do that, dear, come with me."

I slipped out of bed and took her hand. We walked into the kitchen, and as soon as I rounded the corner, I saw Chase standing next to Yuslan.

The look on his face was of genuine concern, and suddenly, I felt terrible for ignoring him for so long. I had plenty of things I wanted to say to him, but all I could do was run and leap into his arms. He wrapped them around me so tightly as we embraced, and once again, his intoxicating scent transfixed me.

We stood like that in the kitchen for several minutes, and I finally came to terms with the fact that I was pregnant with Chase's child.

18

Chase

Feeling Margo in my arms again brought me so much joy. All I wanted to do was hold onto her, terrified that I'd lose her all over again. I kept thinking about all the times I banged on her door, begging and pleading for her to open up. All of the unread text messages, unanswered phone calls, and unreturned voicemails were finally a thing of the past. Margo was back in my arms, and as I kept rocking her back and forth, I told myself that I would never let her go.

But we also had a lot of catching up to do.

Guadalupe and Yuslan left the kitchen, allowing Margo and I to chat for a bit. As she took the seat next to me at the table, I continued to hold her hand and stroke her hair.

She looked up at me and smiled, once again revealing those gorgeous eyes of hers. "I have a ridiculous question to ask you, Chase."

"There's no such thing as a silly question, Margo. Shoot."

"What, exactly, do you do for a living? I mean, I know you're considered a tech titan, but what does that even really mean?"

I chuckled while nodding, understanding why she'd be confused. "Well, I guess tech titan would be a good term. I own a company that sells electronic products—laptops, televisions, home security systems. I travel a lot because we sell our products all over the world."

"Oh, wow. I didn't realize your job was that involved."

I shrugged and kissed the top of her head. "It can be stressful at times, but I truly enjoy what I do. In fact, right before we met, a neighbor reached out and thanked me for my security system. It helped stop an intruder from breaking into his home."

Margo nodded while leaning her head onto my shoulder.

"Enough about me, though, Margo. Tell me more about your job."

"Well," she replied, "I'm a beautician. I do everything from cutting and coloring hair, makeup, facial waxing, and whatever people need to look their best. It's not as exciting as your job sounds, though."

I laughed while stroking her hair. "Believe me, I've nearly fallen asleep on several conference calls. Running a big company isn't as glamorous as people think."

"I know you make electronic products but tell me more about it."

Women had always been more interested in how much I made than what I actually did, once again proving why I was so attracted to Margo.

"Our bestseller is the laptop. It's built so well that it'd be almost impossible to hack, and we've had very few complaints about it. I am a bit concerned about our line of televisions, though. They're not doing quite as well in the market, but with some new features coming out soon, we hope to regain more of the market share."

Margo became disturbingly quiet, almost as though she were pulling away from me again.

"I see," she whispered.

"So, uh, as I was saying, that's pretty much what I do. And yes, it does pay—"

Margo was now crying, which completely threw me for a loop.

Why is she upset about what I do for a living? That doesn't make any sense!

I simply held her hand for several minutes, realizing that it had nothing to do with my work line. Whatever had her upset, was directly related to being absent from work.

"What's wrong, Margo? I hate seeing you so upset." I stroked her hair and kissed her temple, hoping she'd open up. "Please tell me! Just be open and honest with me..."

"I can't believe I didn't even know what you did for work, Chase."

If I ended up being one of her biggest regrets, it would be an emotional burden that I'd carry with me for the rest of my life. "Margo, please tell me what's wrong."

She just continued to shake her head, crying into her palms. I kept thinking back to the first time we had made love, out on the beach, as the waves crashed against that giant rock and underneath a full moon. Was it possible that she regretted having her first time be with me? Or maybe she regretted everything she'd done with me and the upheaval it had caused in her life.

I ran my hands through my hair, thinking that could very well be the case. After all, Margo had been saving her virginity and was in her early twenties. And the first guy she had slept with was forbidden to date her because of her best friend, no less. If I were a woman, I could see why that would be upsetting.

I held her close, but she pulled away, got up and sat across the table from me. Feeling her remove herself killed me inside, but I thought about what Yuslan had said back at her apartment.

Sometimes, all you need to do is give a woman a bit of time, even if that does grind your gears.

It wasn't easy, but I stopped myself from moving and sitting right next to her. If space was what she needed, then I had to respect her decision.

I wouldn't stop asking her to tell me what was wrong, though. "Margo, I promise that whatever is wrong—be it between us or something else—there's nothing you can say or do that would push me away. So please, just tell me what's going on so we can fix it. I'm here for you, and I'll always be here for you!"

"It's nothing, Chase. It's just been a long week for me."

"I can tell something else is going on, Margo. Whatever Ginger has said to you about me isn't true! I'm a good, honest, hard-working man you can trust."

"No, Chase, I—"

"Margo, please! You're killing me."

She finally looked up, directly into my eyes, and I realized that I was wrong. She wasn't upset about her giving me her virginity or my sister or any other petty thought that might have crossed my mind. Whatever was bothering her was the same reason she hadn't been at work all week.

Margo took a long, deep breath, and finally, spat it out. "I'm pregnant, Chase."

Everything around me came to a grinding halt. I was no longer even remotely concerned about work, couldn't care less about gaining a more significant market share with our televisions, and had nearly forgotten that I was still mad at Ginger.

Complete and utter joy filled my cup to overflowing.

Going forward, I would no longer be upset about coming home to a big, empty house. Margo and I would be together with a baby on the way. Sure, we still had to work out the living arrangements since it was still so early in our relationship, but I had never experienced true happiness until that moment. Images of her waiting for me on the other side of the door, right as I opened it while carrying luggage, and holding our baby—there was nothing about that scenario that didn't make my heart soar.

This was what I had been missing in my life.

I ran over and sat down next to her, cradling her hand with mine, wanting to do everything in my power to make her feel better about our unexpected situation. But just as I was about to smile and tell Margo how excited I was, she went back to being an emotional wreck.

"I didn't know how to tell you, Chase." She swallowed hard, dropped her eyes for a moment, and then once again met my gaze. "And there's something else I need to tell you. I overheard your entire conversation with Ginger that day you left my apartment. Remember when you yelled, 'Fine! You want me to stop seeing Margo? Is that what you want?' And then I'll never forget her tone when she replied, 'Yes, that's exactly what I want.'"

Why didn't she hear the rest of our conversation?

"Margo, you didn't hear what I said to Ginger right—"

In between crying hysterically, she kept on talking. "I don't need your money, Chase, and I completely understand if you're not ready to be a father. I can't even imagine what you're thinking right now," she blubbered, and her eyes turned red. "You came over here expecting use to work things out, and then—*surprise*! You're going to be a father!" She tossed her hands into the air and then slumped her shoulders when her hands landed in her lap.

"Margo, you have it all—"

"I'm so sorry, Chase, but I can't do this anymore. I am

emotionally drained and can't even think straight!"

And just like that, Margo ran out of the kitchen and slammed the door to the guest bedroom.

I stood up and waited for a few moments, wondering what I should do. On the one hand, Yuslan's words had gotten through to me, and I finally understood that sometimes you have to let women be alone. But on the other hand, Margo was utterly wrong about how I'd handle the situation.

I walked around the table and tried to run after her. Instead, I nearly ran into Yuslan. I knew he wanted me to let Margo be, but it tore me up inside, just knowing what was going through her mind. I could already foresee several more weeks of unopened text messages, unanswered phone calls, and unreturned voicemails. I pictured myself pounding on her door, whether at their house or her apartment, begging to be let inside. All of my upcoming business trips would, once again, end with me coming back to an empty house.

I refuse to let that happen.

I stared down at Yuslan, who was several inches shorter than me. I had never been one to be disrespectful to my elders, but he was standing in my way.

"You're not going to prevent me from going after her!"

Yuslan didn't say a word back to me, though. Instead, he pounded on his chest with a closed fist and led me out the front door. I had no choice but to follow him, seeing as how it was his house.

By the time I got outside, rage consumed me, but I no longer knew who I was angry with.

19

Margo

After taking a colder shower than usual that morning —which somehow helped with my morning sickness—I forced myself to get ready for work. My baby bump wasn't obvious yet, so thankfully I could still fit into my favorite white crochet dress. Although when I looked at myself from the side, a small bump was starting to show. To my knowledge, Guadalupe and Yuslan were the only ones at the spa who knew I was pregnant.

And I intended to keep it that way until I had no other choice than to make an announcement.

My silk panties were starting to feel a little too tight, so I made a mental note to pick up some new ones after work that evening.

There's another expense I hadn't planned for.

I always knew that being pregnant wasn't a walk in the park, but my body was going through so many changes that I had a hard time keeping up. Sometimes I would burst out crying for no reason, like the night before at dinner. Guadalupe had prepared a delicious grilled chicken dinner, and about halfway into my second helping of mashed potatoes, the tears started flowing. Yuslan gave me a sympathetic, knowing look while Guadalupe rubbed my shoulders.

And all I could do was repeatedly ask why I was crying. That's when Guadalupe reminded me that it was hormones, plain and simple. In other words, I'd better get used to these mood swings because they'll come and go until the baby is born.

That'll be fun to experience while working on clients.

As I looked at myself from the side once more, I couldn't help but smile a little bit. Even though my life had turned upside down, growing a baby inside my body humbled me. Guadalupe said that before I knew it, I'd be feeling it kick and talking to it whenever I had a chance. It pained me to know that she and Yuslan had never been able to have children.

She would always be a mother to me, though.

Right as I sat down to do my makeup, Guadalupe poked her head into the room.

"What are you doing, Margo? Why aren't you back in pajamas? I heard the shower running and thought it was odd that you were up so early."

I sprawled out my makeup and tried to decide on a look for that day. "Getting ready for work. I should have been back at the spa a while ago. It's selfish of me to ask others to pick up my clients."

She came in and sat down on the edge of the bed, watching me in the mirror on her antique vanity. "You shouldn't be worried about work right now, dear. You can have as much time as you'd like just to stay here and collect your thoughts. We have plenty of ladies who are more than willing to help out right now."

I pressed the nude lip liner along my bottom lip, wondering if it was a dark enough shade for the dress I was wearing. "I appreciate that, but I need something to do. There's no point in me sitting around and feeling sorry for myself, plus I need to make money." I looked down at my belly, then back up at Guadalupe. "I have to find some way to provide for the child growing inside of me."

She continued to watch me apply my makeup, and within a few minutes, both of us turned around upon hearing Ginger's voice.

"Margo? Margo, where are you?"

The sound of Ginger's voice made me suddenly very nauseous. Guadalupe and I shot each other a look. Once I was able to suppress the urge to vomit all over her gorgeous rug, I could speak again.

"Wait. What? Is that really, Ginger?"

What the hell is she doing here?

The bedroom door flung open, and there was Ginger, staring back at both of us. Guadalupe shot her a nasty look, and I actually pictured daggers shooting out of her eyes toward Ginger. Before that look, Ginger sounded a bit too excited to be seeing me that morning. I kept thinking about the nasty way she had told Chase to stay away from me and how much I missed our friendship.

Ginger started to say something, but Guadalupe's glare froze her right in her tracks.

For several long, uncomfortable moments, the three of us just stared at each other. Guadalupe was livid, Ginger was excited, and I just wanted to hide under the covers.

"I'll be just down the hallway if anyone needs anything," Guadalupe said while leaving the room. But before she made it to the door, she stared hard enough into Ginger's eyes to get her point across.

As soon as Guadalupe shut the door, Ginger walked closer to me and raked me over with her eyes, squinting them hard as if she were piercing into my soul. "You're pregnant, aren't you, Margo?"

All I could do was nod.

"It's with my brother, isn't it?"

Once again, the only thing I was able to do was nod.

Tears formed in Ginger's eyes, and that's when I stood up. For quite some time, I had been preparing for that moment, fully aware that Ginger would lose her mind upon realizing what had happened. It was bad enough that she went off the rails that I had given her big brother, my virginity, but now I was pregnant with his child.

"Ginger, I can't even imagine how you're feeling right now. The looks you shot Chase and me at the wedding reception, followed by you storming out when I told you that I gave him my virginity, and then finally, your big, massive blowout right outside of my apartment. You've made it clear as day that you don't want us seeing each other. But what you need—"

She held up her hands, refusing to let me say another word.

Here we go—another one of Ginger's temper tantrums.

"You have no idea how much I've missed you, Margo. At work, after work, texting each other—everything. I've been filled with so much guilt and regret because I wasn't there for you when you needed me most. Just knowing that you had to hide something as big as a pregnancy from me tears me up."

My mouth fell open, completely surprised at everything Ginger was saying to me. She walked closer, took my hands, and then both of us sat down on the bed, where she continued to pour her heart out.

"I want to explain why I was so adamant that the two of you not be together. I think it's important that you hear it, Margo."

"Of course, Ginger. Please, tell me everything."

"Before Chase met you, he'd only been serious and—to my knowledge—monogamous with one woman—Amber. The details of their relationship aren't important, but he used to be a huge playboy. Chase went after a former friend of mine, and when I say 'former,' it's because he ruined our friendship."

I nodded while continuing to squeeze her hand.

"Anyway, her name was Aurora, and she was like a sister to me. Chase told her she was the one and that he was head over heels in love with her. Until one day, he stopped answering her messages, and she called me asking if something had happened to him. When I got the call, Chase was sitting right next to me."

"What did he say about her?"

"Chase said that he had never intended on being serious with Aurora and that the passion had died. She cried on my shoulder for weeks, until finally, she ended our friendship. She said that she couldn't stand the fact that Chase could show up at any moment while we were together."

I nodded sympathetically. "Well, I can understand why she felt that way. But it's a shame that he ruined your friendship because of a playboy moment."

Ginger shook her head at me. "There were a lot of other ones, too, Margo. Chase slept with one of my college roommates after dating her for a few weeks. Before it happened, he kept telling her that she was 'the one,' and the two of us had spent several nights planning her wedding. Suffice it to say, Chase ghosted her a week after they slept together. I had to listen to both of them talking about the other one after it happened, too. Chase was defensive, while my roommate was an emotional mess."

I continued to nod, wanting her to finish before I said anything.

"There were several other instances, but one, in particular, has always stuck with me. After the whole Amber situation, Chase went out with my childhood best friend, Courtney. She and I had been inseparable since kindergarten, and he had always flirted with her growing up. One night, while we were all watching a movie at my apartment, the two of them snuck off and had sex in the laundry room."

I scrunched my nose. "That's not very romantic."

"They did it on top of the washer, too. Anyway, I didn't know Chase and Courtney had been dating each other up until that point. Right after it happened, he went home, and she told me that she was in love. The next morning I woke up to a text message from Chase, asking me to break it off with Courtney on his behalf."

I could feel the color draining from my face. "You didn't do it, did you?"

Ginger threw her hands into the air. "How could I not, Margo? If Chase had done it, he would have either been mean or sugarcoated it so much that it gave her hope. And that's when she stopped talking to me, too. So as you can see, this isn't the first time I've been in this situation, and it's why I didn't want the two of you dating. Not because I was jealous of him, but I didn't want to lose my best friend... again."

The two of us hugged for several long minutes, both of us crying on each other's shoulders. Everything was starting to make sense now. When we pulled away from each other, I reassured Ginger that we were okay.

"I can't thank you enough for your protection, Ginger. But it really wasn't necessary. Even if Chase had treated me the same way as those other girls, I wouldn't have let it come between the two of us. Besides, I'm a grown woman who can make her own decisions."

Ginger snickered at me. "That's exactly what Chase said to me that night."

"What night?"

"When Chase and I ran into each other as he was leaving your apartment."

I racked my brain, trying to remember everything they had said to each other. "No, I overheard the entire conversation, Ginger, and he never said that to you."

She shot me a surprised look. "Yes, he did. Right after our big blowout, where he asked if I wanted him to stop seeing you, he laid right into me. He pretty much said he was a grown man and to stay out of his life. And to be honest, Margo, I'd never seen him act that way with any other woman. I've never seen him so happy with someone before, and I sure as hell didn't realize how serious you two were until that night."

I leaned back on the bed as I realized that I had been wrong all along. Chase never had any intention of staying away from me. Regardless of what Ginger said or did, he was going to continue dating me.

"Oh my gosh, Ginger. I've been wrong this entire time!"

We embraced each other again, crying on each other's shoulders as everything fell into place.

"We're seriously overdue for some hangout time, Margo."

"Well, it's going to have to wait. Because I have to go see a man about a baby."

Ginger clapped her hands enthusiastically while smiling from ear to ear. "I can't believe I'm going to be an aunt!"

I grabbed her hand and helped her to her feet. "I need your help, Ginger."

20

Chase

My private stretch of beach in Key Biscayne felt a little too quiet that morning. As I dug my feet into the sand, watching the sunrise, I repeatedly asked myself what I was doing with my life. My yacht was sitting at my dock, practically begging to go out onto the ocean. I had spent dozens of afternoons on it, just enjoying the day while getting some much-needed rest.

And yet as I sat there looking at it, all I could think about was selling the damn thing.

My large, expansive, Spanish-style mansion was custom built and equipped with everything I could ever need. I had top-of-the-line kitchen appliances, the most comfortable mattress money could buy, and the biggest televisions on the market. And if I ever came across something I didn't have, I wouldn't even blink while purchasing it. My entire home was full of high-tech gadgets I barely used, anyway. Surely I could put my money to better use.

There was no point in having all of this stuff when I had nobody to share it with, and that was precisely what would happen.

I was going right back to the life that I had hated so much. Long flights, where I knew I'd open the door to an empty home. Drifting away aimlessly on a yacht, all alone as I tried to clear my mind. None of it mattered to me anymore. I might as well spend the rest of my days holed up in a tiny, one-bedroom apartment while sending Margo child support payments every month. Why did I even bother buying such a big house when it was just for myself, anyway?

I kicked the sand with my feet as I made my way back inside. Beaches were for families to spend time with each other, where kids could build sandcastles while their parents recorded it with their cellphones. What was I—a guy with no family—doing with so many material things anyway? What did I need a private stretch of beach for?

As I poured myself a cup of coffee and looked around my massive kitchen, I thought about just selling the place. It seemed stupid to have so much space for one person. My kitchen had two ovens, two refrigerators, an island with stools, and a soapstone sink that never got used because everything I ate came in a wrapper. I even had a wine refrigerator that never got used because I rarely drank wine.

Maybe I should purchase something much smaller in Orlando or Tampa. A place small enough for a solo existence.

I sank into my oversized couch and turned on the television. I usually appreciated the eighty-inch screen in the vast living room, but it suddenly felt obtrusive and obnoxious. Who the hell needed eighty inches just to watch the news, anyway? I could watch television from a small bed or a television half the size. All it did was make the news anchors' heads look big and funny. Plus, the speakers I had built into my walls were unnecessary. I didn't need to be able to hear what was on the television from across the room.

I flicked off the television and walked into my dining room.

The dining room table and chairs were custom made, yet I had never even eaten a meal at it.

Why did I get a dining room set with a dozen chairs?

I gulped the rest of my coffee, barely wincing as the piping-hot fluid went down my throat. I found myself getting angry at my mansion and all that it stood for. People were starving in the world, and instead of helping them out, I had built a mansion with room for a dozen but only for myself.

It was time to sell that place.

I made my way upstairs and decided to take a cold shower, which had always been my way of pulling myself out of a slump. I started taking them back in college when I had to pull all-nighters just to pass an exam the following day. As the water hit my face, causing me to shudder at the frigid temperature, I had a revelation.

I needed to go after Margo.

Yuslan had given me plenty of good advice, but enough was enough. Margo was carrying my child, for crying out loud, and I refused to be one of those deadbeat dads! Several of my friends had become those types of fathers. It was disgusting to see them be so financially successful while barely contributing anything other than money to their child's life. They needed to get their heads out of their asses before it was too late and their children grew up to resent their fathers.

It pained me inside just to think about our child growing up with little to no contact with me. Once I got through to Margo, then I was sure we could work out an arrangement.

But I didn't want an *arrangement*. I wanted to be with Margo and raise our baby.

I kept thinking about the men I knew who merely sent child support every month and then acted as though that were enough. A child needs a father, a partner to their mother. I wanted to be there for their first word, first step, first haircut...first everything.

I slammed the water off and decided I'd go after Margo, once and for all. If Yuslan and Guadalupe wouldn't let me in their house, I'd climb through the guest bedroom window.

I dried off, slid into a pair of jeans and a black T-shirt, and made my way down the stairs when someone jammed a key into my lock. Before I could access my security system, I heard Ginger's voice.

Oh, hell, no! I am not in the mood for her drama today!

My hand gripped the handrail, prepared to tell Ginger to

go home. After everything she had put me through, I couldn't believe that she had the audacity to let herself into my home. I made a mental note to demand my key back, too, because someone like her sure as hell didn't deserve to have a copy.

As I went to insist that she leave my home, she and Margo walked into my foyer.

It was like looking down at my angel, whose bright smile stared back up at me. Images of the times we'd spent together flooded my mind, and I knew what I had to do.

Margo waved up at me while smiling, mesmerizing me with her gorgeous eyes. I had never run down the stairs that fast before, nearly tripping over my own two feet, and once she was in front of me, I scooped her up.

I held her for several moments, not wanting to let her go for fear that I'd lose her all over again. Feeling her hair in my face was like being in heaven, and even though I knew Ginger was watching us, I didn't care. Margo and I were together, and nothing in the world could ever stop that again.

Not if I had anything to do with it.

But Margo also needed to hear me plead my case.

I gently let her back down and then stood back a few feet, giving her plenty of room so as not to appear overbearing. Yuslan had made a huge impact on me, and I would never encroach on Margo's space again.

"Look, I have so much respect for you. Knowing that you want to do this on your own without coming after my money speaks volumes about your character, Margo. But that's not what I want. I want to be there for you and the baby during this *whole* pregnancy. I'm going to find you the best doctor, build you the best nursery, and do whatever else we need to do to put you in a better setup for raising a child."

Margo started giggling while nodding her head. It felt amazing to see her so happy, once again, as I tried to forget everything we had been through. It was all falling into place.

"I don't know what your benefits package is like at the spa, but I'm going to take care of all the medical bills. The only thing that I want you to focus on is being happy and healthy. And I mean it, Margo. I don't want you to stress out about a single thing when it comes to your pregnancy. We have so much to do. But that's all right; this is what I have assistants for. I'm sure one of them can get you in right away with the best obstetrician in town. I want to make sure both you and the baby are perfectly healthy!"

In between bouts of laughter, Margo nodded toward Ginger, who was staring at me with her arms folded across her chest.

I looked back at Margo, suddenly worried that she hadn't told my sister the good news yet. "Does she know you're pregnant?"

Margo smiled and nodded. It was hard to tell how Ginger felt about the situation. As usual, she was standing there with a pouty look on her face.

I braced myself for how she'd answer my next question, turning my body to face Ginger, I said, "Well, little sister, how do you feel about it?"

She put her hands on her hips and took a few steps closer

to me. "How do I feel about you knocking up my best friend, or how do I feel about becoming an aunt?"

Oh, thank God!

All three of us came together, right there in my huge foyer, and hugged each other. We all shed a few tears, too, which was abnormal for me. But it was impossible not to become emotional at that moment, especially since my home was finally starting to fill up with love. Not only was Margo back in my life, but so was Ginger. The two of us had been close all of our lives, and even though I would have chosen Margo over our relationship without any hesitation, I was relieved that we were back to normal.

After we pulled away from each other, I looked at Ginger and held out my arms. My little sister jumped right into them, and Margo looked just as relieved as I that we were going to be alright. Just knowing that she was concerned about Ginger and me proved we were meant to be together. Other women I had been with over the years would have reacted differently, but not Margo. She was one in a million.

I finally let go of Ginger, and then I remembered a question I had meant to ask her. "By the way, did you ever call Jorge?"

"Yes, but we can talk about that later on, Chase. I'm going to head on out and let you two, well, get caught up. You've been apart long enough."

We watched her leave my mansion, and as soon as the door shut, Margo ran straight into my arms. The two of us kissed passionately as she wrapped her arms around me. I carried her into my living room and then placed her on my oversized sofa. The same sofa I had spent so many nights on all by myself, watching television and wondering if I'd ever have someone to share my life with. And now I was with Margo on that sofa, getting ready to make love to her. Getting ready to fill her with my seed all over again, because I knew that she and I were meant to be together.

Margo looked utterly breathtaking in that white dress, but it desperately needed to come off. I ran my hands up her legs, slid off her panties, and then she arched her back. As my hands reached around and unzipped her dress, my mouth pulled down the top and exposed her swollen, aching nipples.

I took my time making love to her breasts while slowly undressing her until she was completely naked and in front of me. I stood back and took off my pants, and her eyes widened the moment she saw my swollen cock. The same swollen cock she had surrendered her virginity to not long ago and would soon be back inside of her.

I placed my ripped chest on top of her soft stomach, pressed a button on the sofa's side, and then watched as it turned into a bed. I slowly ran my hands up her legs while positioning my shaft against her pussy, kissing her gently on the lips as I made my way inside her. Both of us moaned as we connected, our bodies moving back and forth as pleasure overcame us.

There was no way I'd be selling my mansion now, not with so many rooms where I wanted to make love to Margo.

Her knees went up to her chest as I pushed us to the

brink of an orgasm, and when it finally happened, both of our heads tilted back as we screamed in pleasure.

We laid there for a few minutes, trying to catch our breath until I rolled over and cradled her head against my chest.

"Thank you," I said to Margo once I regained my composure.

She looked up at me and smiled. "For what?"

"For bringing meaning into my life."

21

Margo

It felt so good to be back in Chase's arms. Occasionally I'd be hard on myself for assuming the worst from him, but all that mattered was that he'd be with me every step of the way. I believed everything he had said in the foyer, too. He would step up to the plate and be the best damn father he could be, come hell or high water. I no longer had to go through this alone, and it wasn't going to be just my baby.

It would be *our* baby.

I was so relieved to see him and Ginger make up, as well. That had weighed just as heavily on my mind as the pregnancy. As much as I was attracted to Chase, I could never come between two siblings. They had been through a lot together, and they seemed so close that it made me want my own siblings. In fact, I was fully prepared to raise the baby on my own just so it wouldn't be a strain on their relationship.

Chase and I agreed that we needed to discuss our situation that night.

We were in a relationship, about to have a baby, and lived relatively far away from each other. There was so much to cover, along with getting to know each other better. Even though I could tell he'd be a fantastic father, I still wanted to know all of his quirks. What made him tick, what was he like first thing in the morning, and so much more. Because a relationship was so much more than loving each other and getting over fights. It was about being able to deal with each other's nuances, and I was sure we both had some.

I also wanted to make it clear that as much as I wanted him in my life, I was an independent woman. I saw all of the money he had, and he needed to know that wasn't why I was dating him.

We decided to sit down at his dining room table, which was one of the most beautiful ones that I had ever seen, and discuss everything: our relationship, building a nursery, doctor appointments, and anything else that we could think of. Neither one of us had ever had a child before, so it would be interesting.

Chase went into the kitchen to get us something to drink. I didn't think much of it until I saw him go to put on a pot of coffee.

"By the way, I can't have any caffeine until after the baby is born."

Chase nodded and immediately replaced it with a bag of decaf. "Nope," I said while chuckling. "Even decaf coffee has caffeine, albeit trace amounts."

After putting away all of the coffee, he pulled out a green tea box and held it out to me. I was about to give him the go-ahead, since I had never heard anything bad about it, before deciding to search the internet just in case. I had only heard good things about green tea over the years, though, which hadn't made me appreciate it anymore. I found the taste to be repulsive.

Still, maybe it'd be good for the fetus and help me with morning sickness. So, I did a Google search to see if pregnant women could consume it.

After seeing the results, I looked up at him and shook my head.

"Apparently, green tea has an enzyme that's linked to birth defects in fetuses. Gosh, Chase. These next few months are going to suck for me in the morning. I've been a daily coffee drinker ever since high school. At least Guadalupe has that herbal tea mixture that helps with my headaches and stomach cramps. Remind me to ask her what that is."

Chase hung his head in front of the refrigerator and hunched over the kitchen island. He looked utterly defeated, as though he had done something wrong that he couldn't take back. He let out a big sigh before looking up at me. "I've already missed so much, Margo. I can't believe my own damn luck that I finally find the woman of my dreams, she's pregnant with our baby, and I've missed some of the most important steps along the way. I should have known you can't have caffeine, let alone coffee before even putting a pot on. And what if you hadn't Googled that information about green tea? All of it would have been my fault!"

Chase leaned back over the counter, continuing to shake his head back and forth. It tore me up inside to see him so upset over something so trivial. I highly doubted that a cup of green tea or coffee—regular or decaf—would have harmed the fetus. We would have found out before making it a daily routine. But it also made me feel good that he was so concerned about my wellbeing.

I stood up and walked over to him, but right before I did, he leaned his head against the refrigerator and sighed again.

"I just hope that I know what I'm doing by the time the baby gets here, Margo. Almost everything comes easy to me, but now that you're pregnant, I'm like a blind man without a seeing-eye dog. I can sell my technology products to people worldwide, develop new software to prevent criminals from hacking into computers, and make a top-of-the-line security system. But I can't even make something for you to drink without it harming the baby."

"Chase, you're forgetting that neither one of us knows what we're doing. This is our first child, so naturally, we're going to make mistakes along the way. Besides, I've heard of some women having a cup of coffee a day while pregnant and it's fine. I'm choosing not to, but I don't think anything bad would have happened if I did."

I wrapped my arms around him, hugging him as hard as I

could while resting my head on his shoulder. Both of us stood there in silence for several minutes, rubbing each other's backs with our hands, and doing our best to reassure the other that it was going to be all right. Hell, this was the first child for both of us, so of course, we were bound to make mistakes along the way.

"I know, but still, I should have known better, Margo. I want everything to be perfect with both your pregnancy and this baby. I don't want anything to go wrong."

I looked up at him and smirked. "Okay, that's just not possible, Chase. You know damn well that mistakes will be made, by both you and me, especially since we're first-time parents. You have got to give yourself some credit!"

I reached into the refrigerator, grabbed a bottle of water for both of us, and then walked with him out into the living room. While holding his hand, I did my best to reassure him that he hadn't missed out on too much. "Chase, I know you feel like you've missed a lot, but you really haven't. The only thing you've missed have been conversations between me, Guadalupe, and her husband Yuslan. That's it, so please stop beating yourself up."

That brought a smile to Chase's face. "They're an awfully nice couple, aren't they?"

My smile widened as I continued to rub his hand. "Not only are they nice, but they're an absolute godsend. Guadalupe has been like my therapist. Whatever I needed while staying at their house, she provided it for me. The two of us spent several nights just talking about life, and even though she's never had children, she gave me so much advice about what to expect as a new mother."

Hearing me talk about Guadalupe that way seemed to upset Chase, almost as though he were jealous. I found it odd because unless it was another man talking with me, he didn't seem like the jealous type.

"I should have been with you that night when you took the pregnancy test. When you had been ill all week, I should have put two and two together and gotten you a test myself. And I should have been holding your hand while we waited for the results."

I squeezed Chase's hand a little bit harder, finally realizing what had been bothering him. "Guadalupe was with me, Chase, so I wasn't alone. She's been a second mother to me ever since I started working at the spa. She's helped me deal with this unexpected pregnancy in so many different ways, and I don't know where I'd be without her. Look, you and I had a few road bumps along the way, but what couple doesn't?"

"That's true," he replied.

"While I wish that things had been slightly different between us at the beginning, there's no point in being upset about it now. It's all in the past, Chase, and we have so much to look forward to." I placed his hand on the outside of my belly. "It won't be long before my stomach gets bigger, and according to Guadalupe, the baby will start kicking pretty soon."

Chase bent down and kissed my belly, then rubbed it with

his hands. "I cannot wait for that to happen, Margo. So, she really seemed to take care of you, huh?"

I nodded while also rubbing my belly.

"Who knows what I would have done if it hadn't been for her. That night that I went to the pharmacy, I discovered it was closed and wanted to burst into tears. I was sick of being sick. Non-stop headaches while trying to work, stomach cramps that had me doubled-over in pain. As much as I missed you, I really needed that mini-vacation at Guadalupe's house."

Chase nodded, leaned forward, and kissed me on the cheek.

"I should get Guadalupe a gift of gratitude. Something that shows how much I really appreciate her and Yuslan. Maybe I'll send them a fruit basket or some gourmet desserts. Ginger tells me how good a baker Guadalupe is, so she'd probably appreciate a cake or pie."

"Actually," I said, "Yuslan has a message for you."

"He does? What is it?"

I leaned forward. "He wants you to know that you can pay both of them back by being a good father to your child."

Chase pulled me into his arms yet again, hugging me tightly while repeatedly kissing the top of my head.

You're going to be an amazing father.

"But if you want to get me a gourmet gift or pie, I'm not going to put up much of a protest. If what they say about pregnancy cravings is true, then I'm in for one hell of a ride.

You should have seen the way I devoured food at their house."

"I'll buy you all of the cakes in the world, Margo."

"Oh, I almost forgot something I wanted you to see." I reached over to my purse, where Chase watched as I pulled out a black and white photograph. He took it from me as I held it out to him.

"Are these what I think they are?"

"Yes. Those are pictures from my first ultrasound to confirm the pregnancy. I know you said you'd get me the best doctor in Miami Beach, but I really like this one. I know you'll like her, too."

Tears formed in his eyes as he studied the images, each one showing the little fetus inside of me. It wasn't long before they ran down his face, and I could honestly say I had never seen him so happy. Regardless of the gender, Chase would become an amazing father.

I couldn't have chosen a better man to have a baby with.

After several minutes of him staring at the pictures in awe, I took his hand to snap him out of his trance.

"We have a lot of ground rules to go over, Chase. This is a first for both of us, and we're still so early in our relationship."

He placed the ultrasound pictures onto the coffee table and then smiled directly into my eyes. "Why don't we talk it over dinner since I never did get that second date?"

22

Chase

Margo and I stayed up all night, talking on the couch. And by talking, I mean she did most of it, which was fine by me, especially after all of the advice from Yuslan. Men and women were very different, and he reminded me that even when you want to interject, you have to let them do their thing.

And that was precisely what I did as Margo made it abundantly clear that she'd be doing this on her own, despite repeatedly reassuring me that I'd be there too.

"Since my schedule at the spa is getting fuller and fuller, I'll probably have to hire a nanny. I don't even know where to begin vetting one, but I can figure that out once I get closer to the due date. Until then, I have to find a way to put a nanny in my apartment. Obviously, a one-bedroom isn't ideal for raising a baby, but I signed a lease and can't afford to break it."

"Don't forget that I'll be helping out," I said while rubbing her shoulders.

She placed her hand over mine. "Oh, I know, Chase. I just think that since we have less than a year before I give birth, we need to have everything in order. With both of us working, especially you with your long hours, we're going to need some kind of help. Naturally, I thought about Guadalupe and Yuslan, but they're still busy running the salon."

Even though she kept saying that she knew I'd be there for the baby, something still felt off. I didn't feel as though she genuinely believed that part, and she was creating this massive net for when I walked out of her life—which I wouldn't do even if someone put a gun to my head.

I was at a loss for words, too scared to approach the subject without upsetting her. And since she was carrying such precious cargo, that was the last thing I wanted to do. I wanted everything to happen at her pace.

So I just let her speak until she was too tired to, at which point, we fell asleep on the couch. It had been an emotionally draining couple of days, and even though my bed was calling my name, I didn't want to disturb her since she had fallen asleep on my chest.

The sunlight woke me up the next morning, shining directly into my eyes. I looked down to see Margo still cuddled up against me, in the same spot, and instantly smiled.

I could wake up to this site for the rest of my life.

A lightbulb went off in my head.

It seemed so perfect to have Margo move in with me. It would make things easier for both of us. I could turn one of the many guest rooms into a nursery, preferably one right next to our master suite, and she could take as much time off after giving birth as she wanted to before going back to work. I loved the idea of her staying at home with our child while I worked, and if necessary, I could always work from home to help out. Plus, it meant I wouldn't miss anything else during her pregnancy and then nothing once the baby was born.

It still pained me to know that I hadn't been with Margo when she took her pregnancy test, though. Guadalupe was, without a doubt, a godsend, but it should have been me. Margo should have contacted me when she was sick with headaches and stomach cramps, and we could have figured it out together. But as Margo pointed out, that was all in the past, and what's done is done. All we could do was move forward.

I thought about those ultrasound pictures, which were sprawled out on the coffee table. It would have been wonderful to have been with her at that appointment, watching the images of the fetus show up on the screen, holding each other's hands the entire time. It was hard for me to see the fetus at first, but when I really focused, that's when I lost it. That's when I saw our baby, looking just like a little bean.

Thankfully, the pictures were facing up, meaning I could

get a glimpse of them without waking Margo. I looked down at them, at our little baby, and realized that it made perfect sense. Margo and I had created it, so why shouldn't we be living together? Then again, maybe I was having these thoughts just because she was pregnant. Would I be asking her to move in if she weren't pregnant with our baby?

I decided not to say anything to her until I was sure of my decision. After all, it wasn't just our relationship that was at stake anymore. She was pregnant with our child, and that made the entire situation more sensitive. If things didn't work out with us and she had to move out, it pained me to think of her raising the baby without me involved all of the time. And I wanted so desperately to be there for both the pregnancy and the delivery. It was hard to believe the two of us had known each other for less than three months.

Still, as I watched her sleeping against my chest, something felt so right about having her move in. Yes, it would be a risky move, but I'd heard of other couples who had moved in together immediately. They say that when you find your soul mate, you instantly know.

And that's how I had felt about Margo for quite some time. I just didn't realize it until that moment, as I looked down at her sleeping on me while carrying my baby. And it wasn't just that I no longer wanted to return from business trips to an empty home.

I wanted to return from business trips to see *Margo* waiting for me, along with our child.

Margo shifted a bit on the couch, and even though my leg

was starting to fall asleep, I didn't move. She slowly started to wake up, but I refused to budge until she opened her eyes. Finally, she looked up at me, both of us feeling groggy, and smiled.

"Good morning," I said as my leg started to go completely numb.

"Good morning. I can't believe we fell asleep on the couch last night."

"It's actually pretty comfortable. I didn't realize that until last night, either. How did you sleep?"

She stretched her arms, but my leg was still numb from where she was leaning on it.

"Really well, actually. It sucks that I can't even have coffee, though, because I could go for a big cup right about now."

"Well, right after you deliver the baby, I'll be sure to get you the biggest latte in all of Miami Beach."

"That sounds like a plan."

Margo rolled over, and I breathed a sigh of relief, albeit not too loudly. As she stood up to go to the bathroom, I shook my leg a few times to get the feeling back. Once it was there, I went into the kitchen to prepare a huge breakfast for us. I didn't always get a chance to cook due to my schedule, but when I did, I pulled out all of the stops.

I usually ate a protein bar first thing in the morning, but I wanted to celebrate. So, I started cooking a feast: scrambled eggs with shredded cheddar cheese, fluffy pancakes made with whole milk, savory sausage links, and crispy bacon. My mouth began to water as I fried up the bacon. I was a bit of a health nut and tried to avoid anything greasy or full of fat, so it wasn't a staple in my diet. However, I did have some in my fridge.

But this was a special occasion, and I planned on savoring every bite of that bacon. I couldn't wait until it was so burnt that I could break it in half and then shove it into my mouth, then wash it all down with some orange juice. Fresh orange juice, too, because we were in Florida.

The sound of the bacon hitting the frying pan was music to my ears. It had been far too long since I'd treated myself to some and made a mental note to thank my assistant for stocking my refrigerator up with a pound of it. It was the good kind, too, that came pre-seasoned. I watched it shrivel up in the pan, counting the minutes until I could practically inhale it. It wouldn't be a pretty sight for Margo to see, but if we were going to make this work, then it was better to have her see my flaws upfront.

About halfway through cooking breakfast, with my mouth watering, I heard a sound from the downstairs bathroom. I stood back from the stove and realized that Margo was sick, and not just a little bit.

It was a full-on regurgitation of everything she had eaten the day before.

I ran to the bathroom and opened the door to find Margo hurling into the toilet. Her gorgeous hair was cascading over the seat, so I got on my knees and held it back while rubbing her back.

"It's okay. Just get all of it up and out of your system."

After throwing up again, she started to speak. "I'm so sorry, but bacon—"

"No need to apologize. Just get it out of your system, all right?"

After several more minutes, Margo flushed the toilet and rinsed out her mouth in the sink. She turned to look at me sitting on the wicker chest. "All I do is ruin stuff these days."

I pulled her onto my lap and held her tightly while slowly rocking back and forth. "You didn't ruin our breakfast, Margo. You could never ruin anything for me."

She smiled at me, and once again, I was mesmerized by her gorgeous eyes. "You're just saying that because I'm pregnant with your baby."

"Nah," I said with a gentle squeeze. "I've felt this way for a long time now, and I mean it, Margo. You're everything to me." After kissing the top of her head, I stood up, sat her down in my place, and went to the door. "I'll be right back with some water for you."

After bringing her a bottle of water, I took the entire pan of frying bacon and chucked it into the ocean. I chuckled as a few seagulls took off toward it, pulling out the bacon pieces since the pan had landed pretty close to shore. A few of them even ate the bacon grease, which made me nauseous.

I was about to go and throw it farther into the ocean, but after the birds took all of the bacon, a massive wave came and washed the frying pan away, bacon grease, and all.

I then went back inside, threw all of the remaining bacon in the refrigerator right into the garbage, and took the half-empty garbage bag out to the can. I even lit an odor-neutralizing candle to get rid of the bacon smell, which tended to linger long after you fried it. Before getting back to the rest of the breakfast, I wiped down the stove and counters to get rid of any bacon grease that had splattered too.

If the smell of bacon made Margo sick, then I wouldn't have it anywhere near the house.

I went back into the kitchen and found Margo sitting on a stool, slowly drinking her bottled water.

"Are you still up for eating pancakes, scrambled eggs with cheese, and some savory sausage links? Because if not, then I'll throw all of this out and make you anything you want. Or we can have food delivered. Or, if you prefer, I can take you out to breakfast."

Margo started laughing at me, which always made me feel better. "The pancakes, eggs, and sausage sound delicious. Thank you." Her stomach growled as I resumed cooking.

"Coming right up, and I definitely want to get some food into you. You're eating for two now."

"You know, I'll probably put on some weight with this pregnancy. And just a heads up, anytime I do gain weight, it goes right to my hips and ass."

"I've always loved curvy women, so I'll be sure to make you plenty of food."

Margo watched me cook in between scrolling on her phone. I didn't ask what she was doing, either. Not once had she given me any reason to be suspicious of her, and I loved that we were opening up to each other so quickly. The longer

I watched her sitting at the counter, the more I realized that I would do whatever it took to make her feel comfortable in my home. Because before this pregnancy was over, it would no longer be just *my* house.

It would be *our* home.

23

Margo

Ginger joined me in the break room just a few minutes after I sat down. She eyed my double cheeseburger value meal with envy while opening up the top of her salad. I probably should have gone with a healthier option, even if it meant eating two large salads since I was always hungry, but my cravings always got the best of me. And just as I had expected, my hips and butt were starting to spread out.

"I cannot wait until I'm pregnant, Margo. I'm going to eat everything in sight. Do you know how long it's been since I had a cheeseburger?"

I savored every bite of my juicy burger and cheese fries, before washing it all down with a strawberry milkshake.

"Believe me, Ginger, this barely makes up for all of the aches and pains that come along with being pregnant. The week I took the pregnancy test had been a living hell. Nothing but headaches and stomach cramps. And while I do take full advantage of being able to eat for two, I'd give it up in a heartbeat just to be able to drink coffee again."

"That's a good point," she said while pouring fat-free Italian dressing onto her salad. "Although I must say, you have that perfect pregnancy glow."

"Even as I'm shoveling greasy fast food into my mouth?"

Ginger laughed while taking a bite of her salad. "Yep, it comes naturally to you, Margo. How are things going with Chase, by the way?"

Just hearing his name instantly lifted my mood. "You wouldn't believe how courteous he's been to me. Whatever I want, he gets for me. For example, the other night, I had this massive craving for fried chicken and mashed potatoes at one o'clock in the morning. I kept trying to go back to sleep, but I couldn't focus on anything other than fried chicken and mashed potatoes. So I went downstairs, and Chase came down a few minutes later. Apparently, I was quite noisy."

Ginger giggled.

"What did he say?"

"He told me to relax on the couch, and he'd go pick some up. It was too late to have food delivered, but he knows of a place in downtown Miami Beach that's open all the time. And let me tell you, that was the *best* fried chicken and mashed potatoes I've ever had!"

"That's so funny!"

"Which reminds me, I completely forgot to tell you about the bacon incident. Apparently, I can't stand the smell of bacon, so one morning as he was frying some, I got violently sick in the bathroom. After making sure I was okay, he chucked the frying pan along with the bacon right into the ocean!"

"Oh my God," Ginger gasped.

"He said a bunch of seagulls got to the bacon before the pan got swept away by a huge wave."

Both of us burst out laughing as we pictured him throwing the pan.

"Well, I'm just so thrilled that you two are happy."

I poked around the bottom of my French fry container, looking for any last crumbs.

"By the way, have you heard anything else from Jorge? I remember you saying that Chase gave you his number."

"Oh yeah," Ginger replied. "But he's still in Antwerp, so he's a great person to chat with without worrying about getting too attached. He's also involved with a woman, so needless to say, we're just friends. Oh, and he's having some issues with his business partner. A lot of drama on his end, which makes for some interesting conversations."

"That's great," I said as a few more people walked into the break room. "You can never have enough friends. And between you and me, I've seen pictures of Jorge, and he's alto, oscuro y guapo!"

Ginger laughed so hard that a few of the other employees

looked over at us. "I knew you were going to say that. Guadalupe has planted a bug in your ear. But he's definitely just a friend. Plus, he's super supportive of me finishing my degree."

"That's wonderful," I said while eyeing some of the other employees in the break room. It was a great place to work, but I also didn't want to feed the rumor mill. Every place of employment has people who tend to gossip, and the spa was no different.

"Yeah, and I can't wait to finish my degree too. I am just so sick and tired of doing homework. It feels like an extension of high school, only this time I'm paying thousands of dollars to do all of this work. At least my job here isn't too stressful."

I nodded while thinking about a client from earlier that day. "Ugh, that one woman who wanted her entire face waxed. She knew damn well that it would hurt, and not even halfway through the procedure, she kept threatening to have me fired."

"What an idiot! Who requests their hair be waxed off and then threatens to complain because it hurt?"

I shrugged while drinking the rest of my milkshake, letting it flow all the way down to my stomach. Then I patted my belly, a subtle form of letting the baby know that I had devoured all of that delicious food for both of us.

"I've meant to ask you," Ginger said. "I hope that I'm not stepping on any toes, but what are you and Chase going to do after the baby arrives?"

"What do you mean?"

"Well, you live kind of far away from each other. How will it work? Are you going to bounce the baby back and forth? Because if you are, that means you'll have to do two nurseries."

I nodded while slowly processing that information.

"Have you and Chase discussed any of this stuff?"

"Well, we probably should have by now, but of course we haven't. Oh God, Ginger. There's so much for us to do. We've only talked about things to reassure me that he's going to be by my side. I mean, he keeps saying he'll be there no matter what, and I do believe him. But I'm always looking for reassurance. What if he's only here because I'm pregnant and not because he cares about me?"

Ginger took a long sip of her water before responding, "Well, what have you two been doing lately?"

"Most of the time, we just hang out at his place. It's easier that way instead of going to a restaurant, where I won't have to worry about anyone ordering bacon and then me hurling all over the table. He cooks food that's easy on my stomach, too. For example, pancakes and fried chicken."

Ginger tilted her head at me. "*That's* easy on your stomach, girl?"

I shrugged while smiling at her. "Hey, I keep it down, and it tastes great! But we only talk about light stuff, never anything too involved. Honestly, I'm kind of scared to bring it up. Everything's been going so well for us lately, and I don't want to rock the boat too much while we are getting to know each other better."

A few other employees were looking in our direction by that time, so we lowered our voices a little bit.

"Well, it's something the two of you should probably discuss. You seem happy with each other, so I say just rip off the bandage."

I leaned back in my chair and thought about what she was saying. Ginger was right. It's a conversation that we'd have to have at some point, so we might as well get it out of the way now. I just dreaded having to be the one who mentions it first.

Realizing that I was starting to freak out, Ginger reached across the table and rubbed my hand. "It's an essential conversation, Margo. But it doesn't have to be scary. For example, maybe you can get an apartment that's much closer to Chase's house."

I shook my head while sliding deeper into my chair. "I have a one-year lease on my apartment, and I can't afford to break it."

She rolled her eyes. "Oh, come on, Margo. You know damn well that Chase wouldn't even hesitate to take care of that bill. Even if you don't want to get an apartment, then why not move into Chase's guest house?"

I wrinkled my nose at her. "But Chase doesn't have a guest house, silly. Which rich guy are you talking about?"

Ginger waved her hand in the air. "Just like he wouldn't hesitate to pay off breaking your lease, he can get a guest house built at the drop of a hat. That's not even an issue. The only issue is how you two will raise this baby when you live so far away from each other. Plus, wouldn't you want to be closer to Chase?"

"Of course I do, Ginger, but isn't it too soon?"

"Pfft, I don't think so. You two are so obviously made for each other. I see the way you look at him and the way he looks at you. I think you should seriously consider having him build a guest house. It'll give you space as you continue getting to know each other while building your relationship, yet it'll be close enough to help out whenever you need it."

I just shook my head as we stood up and went back to work. But deep inside, I realized Ginger made a lot of sense. It would be a hell of a lot easier if I lived closer to Chase, and if he had the money to build a guest house, then why not build one? I could pay him to rent it so I didn't feel like I was mooching off of him, and we could raise the baby together while each having our own space.

I went back to my station and got ready for my next client, but all I could think about was my situation with Chase. Ginger had brought up several good points, but Chase and I had just started dating. Sure, our pregnancy situation wasn't ideal, but that didn't mean we should rush things between us.

My next client sat down in my chair, but even as she told me what she wanted done to her hair, all I could think about was what life would be like for our son or daughter. I'd have to hire a nanny to take care of him or her whenever I was at work, not to mention Chase worked upward of sixteen hours a day most of the time. I wanted him to be a part of the child's life, but something would have to change in the near future.

"So," my client said, "if you could take a little bit off the ends so that it rests directly on my shoulders, that would be great."

I nodded while proceeding to wash her hair, hoping she didn't want anything else because I sure as hell wasn't listening. She started talking about her daughter, saying that she had just found out that she was pregnant.

"That's wonderful," I said while scrubbing her scalp.

"She and her husband have been trying for a long time too. It's a blessing. I'm just thankful she's not having a baby out of wedlock, if you know what I mean."

"Well, yes, I know what that means."

My client smiled, realizing that she may have crossed a line, even though my stomach wasn't showing too much yet.

"All that matters is that the parents show the baby plenty of love, but at the end of the day, it's best to have both of them in the same household. You know?"

I smiled and nodded, thinking about the timing of me getting this woman as a client. Part of me wanted to rip her a part and tell her that just because two people aren't married doesn't mean they can't have a baby together. But I also understood what she was saying.

Just how healthy is it to bounce a baby back and forth between homes?

24

Chase
One Month Later

Margo and I had a date at her apartment. She wanted to cook for me as a way to make up for all of the times I had cooked for her. Even though I protested and said it was the least I could do while she was pregnant, she insisted on cooking us an Italian feast: lasagna, a tossed salad, and blueberry pie. She had wanted to serve tiramisu but couldn't since it contained espresso.

She spoke relentlessly about how much she missed coffee, and I couldn't blame her.

Over dinner, in between talking about our jobs and the weather, I kept looking around her tiny apartment. It wasn't suitable to raise a baby in. There wasn't anything blatantly wrong with it, of course. It had modern appliances and a beautiful bathroom, but it was far too small. There wasn't even room for a nursery, which meant Margo would have to put a crib in her bedroom.

"This lasagna is delicious," I said while trying to make small talk. Both of us had been light on words that evening, and the air was a little bit tense. Not in an angry way, per se, but it was apparent that both of us had something on our minds. And neither one of us wanted to be the first one to bring it up.

"It's Guadalupe's recipe. The secret is fresh Italian herbs."

I nodded while taking another bite and casually looking around.

It was your typical one-bedroom apartment. As soon as you opened the door, you walked into a hallway with a closet on the right. A few feet down and to the right was the kitchen, which was a decent size for one person. The bedroom was next to that, and the living room was on the opposite side. For a single person who just needed a place to sleep at night, it was perfect.

But for a woman about to give birth to a baby who'd need plenty of room to roam around and play, it wouldn't be nearly big enough.

"Did you make the salad dressing from scratch, too?"

Margo proudly nodded while winking at me.

I tried to think about how she would even fit a crib in her bedroom. It wasn't that big to begin with, and the only place would be directly next to the window.

Nope. That's not safe enough for my baby.

If she moved her vanity to the other side of the room, there might be a slight chance of a crib fitting, but it'd be right up against her closet door. That meant that every time she opened the door, she ran the risk of hitting the crib and waking the baby if it were sleeping. Or worse, if the baby was nursing on a bottle and started choking because the crib had accidentally gotten struck.

There's no way that a crib can fit in her bedroom.

"Guadalupe showed me how to chop rosemary so that you release the oils. If you don't do it a certain way, then there's no point in even using it in your dish."

"It'd be just like eating a pine needle," I said while smiling at her.

There was always the possibility that Margo would put the crib in the living room, and then use a baby monitor to keep an eye on our child. I wouldn't mind the baby being in a different room—this apartment complex seemed pretty safe, but not nearly as safe as my mansion. Nobody would be able to get within an inch of her or the baby without going through me and the security system.

Maybe she'll put the crib in the hallway.

As we continued eating dinner, I couldn't help but notice how noisy her upstairs neighbors were. Margo saw me staring at the ceiling, too.

"Yeah, they're nice people, but they throw a lot of parties."

"How late do they stay up?"

"It's Miami Beach, so pretty late. Granted, this complex is

primarily working professionals, but some younger college students constantly throw parties. I can't tell you how many times I've been woken up by them blasting loud music."

I bit my tongue so hard that it nearly fell off. There was simply no way in hell that our child was going to be raised in a tiny, one-bedroom apartment with college kids throwing around-the-clock parties. She would be raised in a home, with both of her parents, with plenty of peace and quiet.

Margo could tell that something was on my mind. "Are you all right, Chase?"

"I'm fine," I lied while giving her a reassuring smile.

I wanted to ask Margo to move in with me, but I also didn't want to corner her. Margo had proven that she didn't respond well to pressure, and why should she? She should do things at her own pace, which included how we progressed in our relationship.

But waking up without her next to me was pure torture.

That morning I had rolled over and went to hold her, only to be greeted by cold sheets. I longed to feel her head on my shoulder every day, peacefully sleeping as the sun began to rise outside of my bedroom window. I wanted to see her look up at me and smile, make a comment about not being able to have coffee, and then watch her get ready for work.

"I can't wait for some of that blueberry pie, especially since blueberries are in season right now," I said, trying to distract her from the silence in the room.

Margo moaned while polishing off the rest of her lasagna.

It reminded me of her moans during sex, and when she saw the look on my face, she giggled.

"Hey, I didn't say anything," I replied while chuckling.

Margo couldn't help but be sexy, though, regardless of what she was doing. She even portrayed sexiness when she walked around my house.

Our house.

"How was work today, Chase?"

I took a longer sip of water than was necessary, just to stall the conversation as much as possible. "It was all right. Nothing too major happened. Same stuff, different day."

She nodded while helping herself to another serving of lasagna.

"Yep. Although, that's not always the case at my job. Every client wants something different, and half of the time, they don't even know what that is."

Both of us burst out laughing, but it wasn't long before it went back to an awkward silence.

The upstairs neighbors were now dancing to what sounded like house music, and it got so loud that our dinner plates started to shake. Margo kept her head focused on her plate, slowly eating as we were forced to listen to music so loud my ears felt like they'd start bleeding. I kept thinking about our baby growing up in that apartment, even if it was just for the first year or two. Poor Margo and the baby would get woken up at all hours of the night, and I'd be at home, all alone in an oversized bed.

"Is something on your mind, Margo? You seem a little quiet tonight."

"Nope, just focusing on my food. This pregnancy has been giving me crazy cravings lately."

Even though I wasn't hungry anymore, I put another slice of lasagna onto my plate and slowly forced myself to eat it. The two of us sat in silence for a while, and when I couldn't bring myself to eat anymore, I folded my napkin on the table. "Well, I am officially full. That blueberry pie will have to wait until later on this evening."

"Speak for yourself," Margo said while taking her fork and biting right into the pie. Both of us giggled as she devoured it, then rubbed her belly. "I do that to tell the little one that it's for both of us."

Hearing her call our baby "little one" tugged at my heartstrings, and I couldn't take it anymore. Not to mention the dancing was so intense that the water in our glasses was starting to shake.

As Margo put down her fork a few minutes later, I decided just to spell it out.

"All right, it's time we address the big elephant in the room, Margo."

She gave me a surprised look, but I could tell that it wasn't genuine. "What are you talking about?"

I smiled, reassuring her that it was okay. "Look, you and I both know what's not being said, Margo, so I'm just going to come right out and say it. Would—"

"Maybe we could build that guesthouse, and I could help pay for some of it!"

Her words stopped me dead in my tracks. I leaned back in my chair and stared at her in bewilderment, wondering what the hell she was even talking about. Not once during our relationship did I ever mention building a guest house. In fact, that had never been on my to-do list. Anyone visiting me could stay in any of my guest bedrooms.

"Margo, what in the world are you talking about?" I chuckled after asking her, hoping to ease the tension in the room.

She simply groaned while putting her head in her hands. "A few weeks back, Ginger and I were talking in the break room at work. She mentioned that you and I should be discussing our living arrangements, and you know what? She's right, Chase. I just can't hold this in anymore, and it's been eating at me ever since that day."

"Margo, I want you to be able to speak to me whenever something's on your mind. And don't think for one second that I'm going to run. If anything that matters to me right now, it is your comfort, no matter the circumstance."

Tears formed in her eyes as she smiled. "Do you really mean that, Chase?"

I nodded. "Of course I do, Margo. Why wouldn't I? And I'm not just with you because you're pregnant, either. I'm with you because I *want* to be with you. I'm with you because you are the person I'm supposed to be with. And I genuinely mean that."

The two of us held each other's hands for a while, reassuring each other that we weren't going anywhere. A huge smile formed on her face.

"You have no idea how much your words have relaxed me, Chase, because I don't know if bouncing a baby between two places is all that healthy. But I want your opinion. What do you think? And please be completely honest with me."

Feeling relieved at her question, I smiled before taking a seat that was much closer to her. "I could make this sweet, or I could make this short, and I don't think either of us can take sweet right now because it has taken us much too long to ask this question." As tears ran down her face, I kissed the back of each of her hands before blurting out the question. "Margo, will you move in with me?"

"Yes, Chase! I'll move in with you!"

As the two of us embraced, right there at her kitchen table, I slowly moved my face down to her stomach. I rested my chin on her little pouch, thinking about our little one growing inside of her. Everything in my life was coming together. This was exactly what I had been missing: a family. All of my long hours at work would finally mean something. I wouldn't just be making a lot of money because I could but because I had obligations. And maybe my friends who were absentee fathers would take a hint and get more involved in their own children's lives.

The rest of my life was finally slipping into place. I pushed my chin a little farther into Margo's pouch, and for the very first time, I felt the baby move. Tears streamed down my face as I realized that maybe, just maybe, our son or daughter knew that I was next to him or her on the other side.

"I felt that too," Margo said while running her hands through my hair.

I might have become one of the most successful tech titans in the world and had the ability to buy pretty much anything that I wanted, but nothing was better than what I was experiencing in that moment. Margo and the baby were all that mattered to me and would be for the rest of my life.

EPILOGUE

Margo
One Year Later

I slowly opened my eyes and stared up at the wall. It was still hard to believe that Chase and I lived together, and everything had been going so well. Usually, I'd roll over and hug him, but my intuition told me to look at the time. Something felt off, and when my eyes landed on the alarm clock, I realized why: it was eight o'clock in the morning and I was just waking up. Joanna usually woke me up with her crying long before eight, which meant she was probably crying in her nursery.

I jumped out of bed, looked for my slippers, and then stubbed my toe on the edge of the dresser. After yelling a few profanities, I gave up the search for my slippers and settled for Chase's house shoes. He always left them right in front of his dresser, and even though they were considerably larger than mine, they would have to do. My feet had always been unusually cold, which Chase found adorable. Not once since I had moved in did he see me walking around the house without slippers on my feet.

How could I have slept through Joanna crying? Gah, I am the worst mother!

I dashed toward Joanna's nursery, continuing to chastise myself for sleeping through her cries. Every morning she woke me up, and I hated that I couldn't sleep right next to her crib. But Chase reminded me that we were just fine, especially since we had the baby monitor to alert us when we were needed. The moment she let out any kind of noise, I jolted up and out of sleep and was at her crib within seconds. Chase also found that funny, remarking that just because Joanna made a sound didn't mean I needed to check on her.

By the time I got to Joanna's nursery, I was an emotional wreck. All I wanted to do was wrap her in my arms while apologizing profusely, telling her that Mommy would never sleep through her cries again. Ever since I had given birth to her, I was obsessed with doing everything I could to protect her. If it were possible, I would hold her in my arms all the time. Just knowing I hadn't been there for her that morning was killing me.

But when I got to the nursery, I stopped dead in my tracks.

I peered around the doorway, and all I heard was cooing.

My eyes landed on Chase, who was holding Joanna in the air. She looked delighted to be back in the arms of her daddy, and it was clear as day that he was just as happy to be with her. When I moved to Miami Beach after graduating from college, a over a year ago, I never imagined that I could be so utterly happy. And yet there I was watching the love of my life take care of our daughter so I could sleep in a little later.

I leaned against the doorway and stared at them both, not wanting to ruin this precious moment.

The past year had been a whirlwind of changes. Right after moving in with Chase, he did everything he said he would do. He turned the nearest guest bedroom into a nursery and even hired a professional decorator to pull it all together. He took care of all of my doctor appointments, making sure they were scheduled when I didn't have morning sickness and rescheduling them when I just didn't feel like going. Chase didn't like it when I canceled because I was tired, but I reminded him that hormone fluctuations did that to a woman.

Once we knew we were having a girl, we had the nursery painted a soft white with pink trim. The crib I wanted had sold out, so Chase contacted the seller directly and asked that they make me one. At first, they declined, saying that it was a limited edition, but he paid them a pretty penny to have it made. I joked that after spending so much money on a crib, that we'd be passing it down to our future children. Chase may have come from money, but I hadn't, and I repeatedly told him that just because you *have* money doesn't mean you should *spend* money. The custom crib was a good investment, though, and Joanna seemed to enjoy sleeping in it.

Our home was also fully stocked with everything we could ever need. At all hours of the night, we had access to diapers, baby powder, baby formula, and anything else that little Joanna relied upon.

He had even found lotions that I hadn't heard of before, mainly because they were top-of-the-line, and as a result of Joanna never had a diaper rash. Her skin was always baby soft because he researched the very best baby soap and shampoo and then made sure that we had plenty of it on hand. The only thing I wanted was more time with both of them, although we were almost always together. By the time little Joanna was born, I was head over heels in love with Chase Bowers.

He had stepped up to the plate and proven to be the father that she deserved. Sometimes I just sat back and watched the two of them interact. Even though she couldn't talk yet, he was continually talking to her with the hopes that she'd speak earlier than most children. He wanted to see her succeed in life, and often told me what colleges he wanted her to go to. I told him to relax and enjoy her childhood years because they'll go fast.

Chase saw me standing in the doorway. "There's Mommy, Joanna! Do you wanna see Mommy?"

As she blew spit bubbles, Chase handed me our daughter. His voice was enough to bring me out of my trance, and I clutched Joanna tightly to my chest while Chase kissed my cheek. He smelled so good, regardless of the time of the day. I often told him that he had cologne embedded in his DNA.

"Good morning," I said to him.

"Good morning to you, too," he replied while spanking my butt.

It was those small moments of affection that I truly enjoyed about our relationship. The ones in between the more significant romantic gestures, like when Chase sent me roses out of the blue or took me out to dinner. Just knowing that we truly loved each other was enough for me.

The three of us made our way downstairs, where Chase cooked the two of us breakfast, and I nursed Joanna. I loved sitting at the table, watching him cook first thing in the morning. He had that sexy stubble on his face, and seeing him take care of me filled me with love. Chase was also one hell of a chef, and I appreciated that he never had another slice of bacon in the kitchen. He had even sworn not to eat it outside of the house because he didn't want me to have me smell it on his breath.

I had always had a strong sense of smell, too.

Joanna continued to nurse while Chase flipped the pancakes. I didn't know what he did to make them so good, but they were some of the best I had ever had. He said it was because he used fresh whole milk and made the batter from scratch. Whereas I always used the box kind.

It worked for me.

I smiled as Chase put out some fresh fruit to go with our breakfast. He took plenty of notes at our doctor's appointments when I was pregnant, and he often reminded me that as long as I was nursing, it was imperative that I consume as many nutrients as possible. He was constantly having fresh fruit delivered to the house, which I didn't mind. Florida had some of the best fruit I had ever tasted.

He started to plate up the pancakes just as Joanna finished nursing, which was perfect because I was starving. My stomach had been growling since the moment I woke up and only continued to get louder as the smell of pancakes wafted throughout the kitchen.

The great thing about Chase's job is that it allowed him to work from home, and he had been doing that a lot since I gave birth. He always wanted to be on hand to help with the baby. He even told me on numerous occasions that I never had to work again, but of course, I didn't take him up on that offer. Being a beautician had been my lifelong dream, and as soon as Joanna was older, I had every intention of going back to work and rebuilding my clientele. By that time, Chase and I decided that we'd hire a nanny, and of course, he insisted that she'd be the best nanny in the business.

I loved his attention to detail.

As Chase and I sat down to breakfast, I reminded him about the party that evening. "Remember the party tonight, Chase. Guadalupe's throwing a party to celebrate Ginger graduating from college, and all of the spa's clientele will be there too. Plus, Guadalupe wants to celebrate Ginger becoming their new accountant."

"I haven't forgotten. Guadalupe's niece is going to watch Joanna, right?"

"Yep," I said while taking a bite of my pancake. "And don't worry, Guadalupe's niece is fully qualified to take care of her while we're at the party. She's a sweetheart and has all of our contact information."

Chase moved closer to us and smiled, right before kissing the top of my head.

"What's going on," I said while staring at him quizzically.

"I have something for you, Margo."

"Chase, you need to stop buying me gifts. I told you that I'm perfectly happy with everything I have, and I couldn't ask for anything more."

"I beg to differ." Chase pulled out a small velvet box and then nodded at me to open it.

As soon as I did, the biggest, most beautiful diamond ring stared back at me. Tears welled in my eyes as I looked at it and then again at Chase.

"Chase, what is this?"

"Margo, I love you with everything inside of me. In fact, I don't even think 'love' begins to describe how much you mean to me. It pains me to know that our daughter has my last name, but you don't."

I giggled while staring into his mesmerizing eyes. "Well, maybe I'll keep my last name and take the ring anyway."

He held his hands up and laughed back. "Look, as long as you marry me, I don't care what the hell you do with your last name!"

"Wait," I said, "are you serious, Chase? Are you asking me to marry you?"

Chase stood up, took both the baby and me into his arms, and stared into my eyes. "Yes, Margo. That's what I'm asking you. Will you marry me?"

"Yes, Chase! I will marry you! Yes, yes, yes!"

Chase slipped the ring onto my finger and kissed me several times.

"I was waiting for the party day to give you the ring since it'd be the perfect place to show it off. I know it's to celebrate Ginger graduating from college, but she won't mind. Besides, she'll be thrilled that we're getting married."

Both of us burst out laughing, and right at that minute, Chase's phone rang.

As he talked with what sounded like Jorge, I went back to eating my pancakes and nuzzling Joanna.

"Jorge," Chase said into the phone. "What's going on?" Pause. "Oh, really?" Pause. "So, you're back in town and will be at Ginger's graduation party tonight?"

My cellphone went off with a text message alert, and I looked down to see that it was from Ginger.

Ginger: Guess who I just got a text from?

Made in the USA
Las Vegas, NV
08 July 2021

26132866R00118